SUT
1/15

First published by Jacana Media (Pty) Ltd in 2014

10 Orange Street
Sunnyside
Auckland Park 2092
South Africa
+2711 628 3200
www.jacana.co.za

© Thando Mgqolozana, 2014

ISBN 978-1-4314-0952-5

Cover design by
Set in Sabon 11/14.5 pt
Printed and bound by Creda Communications
Job No. 002123

See a complete list of Jacana titles at www.jacana.co.za

Thando Mgqolozana

Disclaimer

Believe it or not, this is a work of fiction. The room

There are people at my door. They came in from the broken side door of the corridor, which is to the right of my room, and they are knocking on mine.

she was looking for.

I stop writing. I am sitting on my single bed, and I am wishing that the knockers would give up and leave. I am observing their feet in the space under the door. The corridor lights are quite bright, and my lamp inside is dim, so I can clearly see the movement of the knockers' feet outside. Usually, if there are four shadows, I know it is the two fluorescent lights above and on either side of the knocker projecting one person's two feet as four shadows. But presently I see many, and they are steadying themselves from one corner of the door to the other.

I have just come back from searching the campus for Pamodi after she left the room, saying she was going to the bathroom. She is gone, running away from me. And now there are people knocking on my door.

When she came in at eight-on-the-head earlier tonight, she'd found me watching *Mr Ibu*. She'd opened the door using the spare key she keeps on her. I'd heard the padlock on my door being opened, and adjusted my mood so that it adjusted my face to say: I'm pissed off.

She'd said, "Hi?" while closing the door behind her.
"Hi, Pamodi."

I'd purposely looked back at the TV, giving her a chance to acquit herself, but she didn't. Instead she sat on the end of the bed, next to where my underwear was hanging, arms folded cheekily. I felt myself coming undone, but made a conscious decision to keep it together. I didn't want a repeat of three weeks ago. I'd said, "Well?" – a polite way to ask where the fuck she'd been. "Well what?" she had said, her eyes rolling upwards.

"You've been away all day!"

"*Hehake*, I went to Poetry."

Where the hell is Poetry? There's no place called Poetry on campus where female students can go for an entire day and half the night in their pyjamas without letting their boyfriends know. I know there's random poetry gigs held at recreation halls in the residences, but those don't last more than an hour, no one is going to organise a poetry gig during an election season, and in any event, I've never known Pamodi to be one for poetry. Calm down, Zizi, breathe, I'd told myself. I kept quiet for a moment, waiting, looking at this selfish person, but she didn't elaborate, so I said, "Poetry?"

"Yes, Melody was performing her new poem tonight." If I had been a good boyfriend – and apparently I'm not – I should have left it there, and we would have started afresh, made love, after which I'd write my presidential manifesto ready to be delivered tomorrow, and she would be here now; but the trouble is that I am a catastrophe of a boyfriend. I was infuriated by her impertinence. I wasn't hearing the apology I was wishing for. She was making no attempt to disarm me, even though my face must have been telling her in unambiguous terms that I was a bomb wanting to be disarmed.

"What's gotten into you, Family..."

"I'm going to my room."

That's when I flew off the bed and went to stop her leaving. I held her by the arm. I admit I may have forcibly turned her away from the door. She said, "You're hurting me!" In fact she screamed it, and on purpose, so my neighbours – whom she knows respect and look up to me – as well as anyone passing in the corridor, would get the impression that yet another female student was being abused by someone she trusted. She knows that most people know that H-14 is my room, and that I am supposed to be exemplary, given my public credentials.

"You're not going anywhere until you tell me what's going on here. If you had any sense in you, you'd know I've been looking for you for hours, and you'd know I've been worried, and you'd try to make me happy, whatever. But you're just being cheeky for no reason, and now, just like that, you say you're going to your room!"

"Can you stop holding me like that, Zizi? You're hurting me!" She'd said it again, and this time she'd tilted her head, making as if her arm was completely removed from her body. Her friends may be amateur poets, but she's the authority on performing hurt. She let the chewing gum slip out of her mouth and fall to the floor, like someone who was in sheer agony, but she couldn't be – I was only holding her by the elbow, and not roughly either, maybe just a little awkwardly. But Pamodi has recently made it her vocation to analyse the violent element in me.

For a few seconds I'd contemplated the idea of letting her go, recomposing myself, getting myself another girlfriend – perhaps someone prettier, sharper, more respectful, with a less complicated background, someone with no ulcerations in her alimentary canal, a reasonably straight jawline, a better-maintained set of hair extensions, someone who knows the purpose of attending university, has read a little bit of Biko, does not think all men must go to the gym, talks less about marriage, doesn't think all kids are cute, a lady generally dignified and worthy of love; in short, anyone but Pamodi – anyone with a sizeable combination of the things Pamodi lacks.

But if I'd let her go, it would have meant she was having her way, she was winning, which I was not about to allow so easily. All I wanted was for her to acknowledge that she had upset me, that she was being unfair, and perhaps should do something about it, but she was blatantly refusing, giving me rotten attitude just because she could.

"Pamodi, I am your boyfriend, why do I need to explain that to you? Why do I have to feel like you're doing me a favour by being with me?" I finally released her arm, and I have to admit I almost threw it back at her.

She shot back, "No, Zizi, you are treating me like I'm your possession."

"My possession?"

"What do you call this?'

clock, plotting to torment me with bizarre questions as soon as I step in. You'd let me live my life on my terms and trust me to return to you, like I just did. You'd stop punishing me for sins I committed before I met you. You'd not be so obsessed with my exes. You'd realise I'm only nineteen. You'd not always be anxious that I'm going to embarrass you by living my life the way I choose. You'd let me be my own person, not an accessory on legs. You'd stop the violence."

"Hang on, wait – this is absurd!"

"That's what I'm saying: it's absurd how you're treating me. I've had no life since I met you. You've made me alienate my friends. I have no personal space. I can't be away from you without feeling that you're following me. I'm falling behind with my studies because I'm emotionally distracted, and I can't even take a nap without you getting all worked up."

"Jesus! You're going crazy!"

"That's another thing: all these labels!"

"Pamodi, you can't lie to me so many times and expect to be trusted. Trust is something you cultivate, and you've managed to erode any little trust I had in you in the shortest space of time. You're playing double standards!"

And what I really wanted to say was, "You don't cheat and expect to be trusted," but I didn't put it that way because, as some people have said of me, I was raised in the homeland – apparently it does something to your vocabulary.

She was doing the talking, accusing me of all sorts of vulgar atrocities, and making predictions about my doomed political future. Some of the things she said stung badly, but some were hilarious. I couldn't laugh, although I was celebrating that I was managing to keep calm, wasn't getting all worked up, and that this was not going to end up with a fight like three weeks ago. She was shouting all right, but the more she spoke, the more I detected some form of guilt in her. She just didn't know how to simmer down and put the fire out. I left her by the door and went to lean on the windowsill, pulling the green curtain aside.

I'd felt a strange thing happen: while my enraged girlfriend stood there, pointing fingers at me and rubbing her supposedly sore elbow, and even though she was wearing that dirty pair of maroon pyjamas that needs to be thoroughly defluffed and Stay-Softened, I'd felt a slow, pulsing erection forming inside my jeans. It was the kind that you know won't end up in a huge jerking flop. The kind of erection any man could rely on.

I thought about moving from the windowsill to go and sit on the bed. If I continued leaning upright, sooner rather than later, Pamodi was going to see the hardness sticking up, nodding like a flagpole. If she did, she would conclude that while we were arguing, while in fact we were at each other's throats, I was mentally stimulating myself. I moved towards the bed while also trying to shield my arousal, which Pamodi

any more, so I wasn't surprised when Pamodi said, "You are unbelievable!"

There was silence.

She came over to stand between my legs and massage my shoulders, which I felt like dropping even lower to unburden myself. I'd held onto her lean thighs, which were harder than I remembered, gripping them from behind. I didn't even think about the pyjamas I hated. She said, "Baby..." for the first time. "I need to pee."

"Okay, Baby. You didn't need to ask me."

"Don't say that. I love you."

"I love you too, Baby."

I'd patted her on the lips. They were dry and chapped. She went to the all-purpose built-in wardrobe with recently varnished brown doors, opened the door, and disappeared behind it.

She'd said, "Do we have toilet paper?"

"Check the bottom."

"Oh, lots..."

She'd closed the wardrobe. Its hinges squeaked from overuse and lack of oil. She began rolling some toilet paper onto her hand, like a bandage. She was not looking at me. I didn't know what to say to her. Things were happening fast. Every moment was a turning point. I didn't think she was being sincere, but the erection had put me in a subjugated position. She could go to Mrs Hubby, the house manager, to report me as having threatened her with violence, mention the incident of three weeks ago, be advised to report me to the Proctor, who would summon me and, if I was lucky, give me my first but perhaps final warning, and instruct me to leave her alone or face automatic expulsion.

Even if I obeyed, the damage would be done: the Proctor would publish my case in the *Student Voice* weekly, together with my sworn apology, which would coincide with our door-to-door campaigns next week before the voting. But before that, all her friends would probably attend my presidential manifesto presentation tomorrow, and they'd ask my "honest opinion" on the scourge of gender-based violence on campus, in the presence of feminists from the Centre for Gender Advocacy. For all those who might have missed the story in the *Student Voice* and the drama at the Student Centre during the presidential manifestos, the opposition's trusted propaganda newsletter, *The Private Eye*, would carry the gory details of what they'd probably call my unrivalled record of domestic violence. No one knows who writes *The Private Eye* – nobody can be prosecuted for defamation – but everyone knows it is someone with incisive analytical abilities, who favours the opposition, and probably writes the best English essays on the entire campus.

I was troubled by this, and it compelled me to call for Pamodi's attention, although not yet knowing how I would say what I wanted. I wanted to ask her to forgive me, to show her how we were ruining each other, and how it was unnecessary and dangerous, ~~and hopefully forget~~

But she didn't look my way. She took a ~~strip~~ of toilet paper off her hand and used it to pick up the chewing gum she'd spat out; then she threw it at the rubbish bin behind the door. She missed by a slight margin and the paper fell on the side, next to the broom. She went to pick it up and threw it at the bin again. She scored. It was a sore reminder of the fight we'd just had. Pamodi's movements were very deliberate, and it seemed she'd resolved to pay attention to me only once she'd finished the critical task of picking the bubblegum off the floor and depositing it in the bin.

"Be quick *ke*, Baby."

"Are you saying something?"

"I was saying I love you."

"I love you too, Baby. I'll be back quick." Her face had none of the fear or anger it had shown not too long ago. Chief of my worries now was that I couldn't account for her change of mood – mine was due to the mass that had randomly gathered itself between my legs – and I was afraid of what might happen. "If Melody calls me, *ne*," she said before she left the room, "tell her I'm in the loo. I'm expecting a call from her. She's coming to pick up her journal that's got her poetry. She left it with me after performing because..."

"She's going to Godfrey?"

She'd laughed for the first time, and left, taking her keys with her, but leaving her phone.

Melody and her Godfrey are a private joke of ours. Theirs is an unusual relationship: whenever Melody feels like it, she rocks up at Godfrey's room in our dorm, Ruth First Residence. But Melody has a problem: her gums bleed while she sleeps, so no matter how much she wants to stay all night, she can't, because, Pamodi told me, all her past, very brief, relationships have ended because of her soft gums. To keep the convenient thing between herself and Godfrey going, she avoids sleeping over. As Pamodi often says, "She's refusing to lose Godfrey over teeth." I'd say, "Literally holding him by the fangs," and we'd roar with laughter.

But those were the witty old days when we had just met, and when just about anything and every non-thing, from the tragic to the comic, was a source of amusement we shared. Things changed quickly, and for the worse, and I don't think either of us can say why we're still together. It is easier to explain reasons for separation than staying. Every time things go bad, our foremost question is why we haven't left each other: but we daren't leave. If we left every time, we'd never know what it feels like to stay. So we make love and park the question. I hoped that as soon as Pamodi came back, we'd do exactly this, again. It was our pattern.

I was encouraged by the hardness of my arousal; this erection felt like it was going to last. But, to be on the safe side, I wanted to be sure it wouldn't give in on me at the crucial moment by exploding untimely. It's what all men worry about when they've not had ~~...~~

decided I was going to do a quick one on my bed with a condom on, which I was hoping to discard before Pamodi came back. Even if the promising hardness didn't turn out to be such a hit, at least I'd have gotten rid of the rushing champs, and that way I could last a little longer than if I hadn't delivered myself. Pamodi had to recognise me in bed if she couldn't do it to my person, and that required a fair amount of durability.

I find my girlfriend's style of walking objectionable. It is a symptom of snobbery one has come to expect from Model-C types. Snobbery is a sickness whose aetiology can be traced to the birth of our freedom. She grew up in the nineties with the country's first bunch of brats, who are not well trained in lifting their feet from the ground when walking. She drags her feet, and it irons my nerves flat. But it makes her easily identifiable if I'm in my room and trying to ascertain who is approaching the door.

So I knew if I put the condom on and did my thing, her bratty drag would tell me when she was approaching down the corridor from the bathrooms, which would mean I'd have time to fold up quickly and erect as innocent a face as I could muster.

To deliver yourself, it is best not to visualise the girl you're about to make love to, because this can mess up your concentration. This is why it is handy to have folders of leisure saved up in your mind. I keep images of girls floating in my head all the time. If you are going to have sex with, say, your girlfriend, you must know a guy from another corridor is possibly featuring in her mind.

This is absolutely true of me and Pamodi: Sthombe, a tall, fair-skinned, very sexy lady with a faulty eye, is a constant presence in our sexual life. Sthombe is famously rumoured to be a prostitute who works by night at Sea Point. I think the correct way to describe Sthombe is liberated. She has a sense of agency, not confined by conventional notions of purity and occupation, which cannot be said about most students of any accessible gender. The prostitution thing is spread around campus by people who lack confidence, who envy her the silver Mercedes convertible she parks on NY 1 every other day, precisely because it's not hers, or theirs. She is a great help at moments when I urgently need to deliver myself. But tonight, Sthombe failed to inspire me – I was too anxious.

I folded in and waited for Pamodi.

I thought I'd hear the toilet door open and close. The hinges of all the doors on this campus need oil. But there was no squeaking. Perhaps she was being gentle with the doors – it was possible if she was in a contemplative mood. But there was no sound of doors opening, or toilet flushing, or Pamodi humming a Methodist hymn, or the taps running as she washed her hands.

This was taking way too long, and when I'd

eventually left the room in search of her, I found the toilet silent. The toilet always tells you if it has had a recent occupant. But this time it told me, with its silence

down, and hers from the knee up

brown skins, his coarse and hairy, and hers looking like it had the right amount of everything it needed. She had a shower cap on and looked like she'd sprung out of a soap advertisement. He was locking the door, and she was holding the toiletry bag, waiting for him. She ran into the bathrooms when she saw me, and they both giggled.

"*Heita*," I said, and he surprised me by replying, "Sure, President."

He also winked, and I wondered if I'd gawked. The Bible cautions against gawking neighbours. I returned to my room and, at first, not knowing what to make of the situation, or what step to take next, and while still cogitating, I'd put on a jacket and proper shoes. Winter has dragged on forever in Cape Town this year, and it was obvious that my girlfriend was on a mission to turn the screws on me some more.

I'd put on my seldom-worn SuperSport jacket with detachable arms, the red laceless sneakers that are easy to wear, and I already had on a faded, unremarkable pair of jeans. As I was picking up my keys, I had the feeling that when I returned, my life would be different. If that happened, I didn't want my bed to be unmade, the TV blurring away, the old manifesto speeches lying uncared for next to the bed. There had to be some kind of order, if not in the world in general, then at least in mine.

I'd decided to go to Pamodi's room. Maybe she had made a detour there while I was psyching myself up for what I thought was going to be our most passionate making-up. We hadn't had sex since the night we fought. It's been three dry weeks. She has been sleeping in her room, spending less and less time with me. She's even resumed reading the Bible before sleeping, like I discovered she did when we'd just met. Nothing is more frightful than when your girlfriend prays about you in her room, and then lets you know about it via a short text message as soon as she finishes.

When I came out, I almost bumped into Madoda, my former roommate. Door H-12 is directly opposite my H-14, exactly a metre away. Before I moved to the single room, I had shared room H-12 with him. Maybe it is the homeland territorial instinct in me, but somehow I still regard room H-12 as mine. Madoda was opening the door of my old room now. He is as blind as an owl in daylight, but he does judo, and is the reigning national youth champion and a Western Province instructor. The first time we met, he asked me within seconds if I played any sport. I'd told him the truth, he giggled, and I was a little ashamed, but I was mostly disappointed that he didn't recognise me, as I'm a public person on this campus. I must have held a grudge against him for that because one day I'd asked him, "So, Roomza, do you do judo with your glasses on?"

"Why, *hlll*?"

"I've never seen you without them."

He'd said he didn't wear them on the platform, but sometimes he walks right past his opponent: "The [illegible] cannot put anything past [illegible] guy who cooked samp mealies – which take about eight hours to boil to perfection on a normal cooking stove – using an old frying pan with no lid on.

That night, I had returned to H-12 after chairing a difficult meeting where our organisation had had to decide whether to go ahead with the planned student protest that was meant to agitate for the arrest, eviction and deportation of Professor Alphonse Nshimirimana of the Department of Pharmacy, who, we had recently learned, had used pharmaceutical apparatus and drugs that belonged to the university to maim Tutsis during the Rwandan genocide in Butare. After a very long discussion, to-ing and fro-ing, we'd decided to consult the provincial leadership of the mother body, not about the correctness of our decision to protest, but about the political implications of such a move in broader society.

We had held the Branch Executive Committee extended meeting, which we simply called The Extended, at the Colleen Williams recreation hall, which is opposite Ruth First. I was chairing. When the motion to consult the mother body had been raised, seconded, and when I'd checked whether there were any objections, and there were none, I'd said, "Comrades, let me summarise and close this meeting…"

"This is going to be interesting," said Sindane, and I'd known he was once again ready to discredit my aptitude, because he was still very bitter that I'd been elected Chairperson of the Branch instead of him. This meant, or so he must have gathered from previous experience, that I was the heir apparent to the position of President of the Student Representative Council. Since losing the political position of Chairperson to me at our elective Annual General Meeting at the end of last year, he had allocated himself the honourable position of number one opponent from within.

I'd nodded to the Branch Secretary to take notes as I spoke, so that my summary was minuted, and had said, "What I am hearing comrades say is that, going forward, a delegation led by the office of the Branch Chair, comprising his Deputy, the Secretary and her Deputy, as well as the Political Commissar, should approach the office of the Provincial Secretary of the mother body to engage him on the merits and demerits of the issue around the Rwandan Professor. On returning, the delegation shall brief the Executive, which will decide whether an Extended shall be called to brief comrades, and later, the masses."

I'd looked at my Branch Secretary, who was minuting the summary word for word, and then across the room: "Is the summary in order, Comrades?"

"Well, Chair, the summary would be correct if…" said Sindane, massaging his well-trimmed goatee, and

I'd interjected, "Sindane, nobody said you can speak."

"But Chair, you just asked the Extended to assist you with the summary."

[text obscured] ... to tell you this one more ...

open your mouth and speak when I give you ... Anything outside those parameters is ill-discipline, and anyone not willing to subject themselves to the guiding principles of this organisation is free to deposit their membership card with the office of the Branch Secretary and leave. This is a political organisation, comrades, not a glorified spaza shop!"

I'd paused to take in some air. "Now, comrades, is the summary a true reflection of the deliberations in this Extended?"

I'd looked around for hands, "Styles, you are noted. Is there any other hand?" And when there was no other hand, I'd told Styles, "Shoot, comrade."

"My comrade Chair, your summary is erudite and succinct. It reminds me why the last AGM unanimously bestowed all its confidence in you. You are the future, comrade Chair. Close the Extended and let these students go study."

I'd said, "Comrade Styles moves for the adoption of the summary as a true reflection of the meeting, anyone seconding that motion?"

"Seconded, Chair," somebody from the far corner said with a tiny voice.

"Who is that?"

There were chuckles, and the speaker turned out to be one of the excitable first-year law students we had recruited to serve as foot soldiers during the last election season. Gently, I had explained the procedure of the Extended once more, and added, perhaps unnecessarily, "Don't learn the bad habits of the likes of Sindane. Now, is there any comrade in this meeting who feels very strongly that, unless altered significantly, the Chair's summary is misleading and could result in some kind of tsunami?"

As expected, Sindane had his hand up.

"Speak, Sindane."

"For starters," he'd said, and began adjusting his horn-rimmed glasses. They had rectangular lenses, which always made his spruce face more prominent than others in groups. "I'd like to thank the Chair for granting me the opportunity to speak in this Extended..."

Whenever Sindane began his comments with "For starters," or "The longs and the shorts", or "In the interest of progress", with an accent that made you forget that he was the son of a taxi-driver from Gugulethu, you knew he wasn't being sincere. At that moment, he'd thanked me for my generosity in granting him the platform, which he said was a blessing because "There are worse dictators in the world". I didn't even reprimand him when he said my summary was "at best semantically impoverished", and at worst, it "betrayed the spirit of solidarity with the people of Rwanda who lie dead in mass graves". I'd decided just before he spoke that the Extended was over, but I'd let him speak to make the point that it is good leadership practice to let your adversaries have the last word – as they don't have anything else.

Then I'd adjourned the meeting.

~~out of the rec hall in single file. A~~

~~spirit when there is political tension.~~

Mr Hubby, the porter, was behind the counter in the foyer. Before I could say anything to him – and I wasn't planning to say much since this guy is famous for talking to students well past midnight about random things – he'd said, "Morning!"

"Morning, Hubby," I'd replied, even though it was night-time, because all three hundred and twenty Ruth First housemates had collectively decided that correcting Hubby's erroneous greetings was rather cruel and unnecessary. Hubby is a nice guy, and the truth is that there are times when his greetings are appropriate – like after midnight.

I'd upped my pace so I could avoid a potentially lengthy conversation with Hubby. If it'd been his wife, Mrs Hubby, I'd probably have chatted, because Mrs Hubby is the official manager of the house, and it doesn't hurt being in her good books, while Hubby is a manager only by association. *The Private Eye* had said that Hubby thought management positions were sexually transmitted, which we all thought was way below the belt, even by the sunken standards of *The Private Eye*.

Nothing prepared me for the disaster at H-12.

When I arrived at the door, I'd decided to knock before I used my key to open the padlock. The last time I had just walked in, Madoda had been busy in my fridge, and he couldn't bring himself to explain to me just what he was up to. So I'd decided to give a warning when I was at the door, so that it didn't look like I was spying on him, which, I should be clear, I wasn't. I generally hate people who snoop around, and given a chance, I'd probably do all I could to catch a thief, but there's something I never want to see again in a black person's face: humiliation. I've seen too much of it in my life, and every time it ends up consuming me. I'm only going to be as humiliating as I choose, and not more than that.

When there was no answer to my knock, I'd opened the door, careful not to make unnecessary noises, and found the main light and our two side lamps off, and my curtains undrawn. In the dark I could see that there was cargo on Madoda's bed, and as soon as I reached for my side lamp and switched it on, I learned that it was no cargo but Madoda himself.

I'd closed my curtains, made myself cereal with cold milk, and deposited the cereal bowl back in my wardrobe that kept not only books, suitcases, toiletries, food, dishes and pots, but clothes and shoes as well. I was ready to nap. If you're hoping to catch some sleep on this campus, it is wise to do so before The Barn closes at three-on-the-head, which is when fellow students return to the residences to recreate The Barn's atmosphere in the corridors.

There are also potential rapists from the neighbouring institution who somehow always find their way into our dorms and start knocking on random doors, in the hope, it seems, that with a little persuasion, a girl from our campus will open the door to them, then perhaps ~~something else. That's the fate of~~

I woke up, I was suffocating ~~from a~~ whose source I initially thought was my odd body, but which turned out to be Madoda's frying pan. There was indeed a plastic fork next to the clock. Our entire room was full of steam. I'd jumped off the bed ready to run, which shocked Madoda awake as he'd covered himself completely with blankets. This while cooking with an open frying pan on the side of his bed.

"Roomza, is there a fire?" he'd asked as he woke up, and I didn't say anything in reply. If it wasn't infuriating, I'd probably have chuckled, but there's no funnies in the threat of death by fire. Nobody tells you when you enrol that university is a halfway house for deadly roommates. I stood there, looking at his side of the room. The frying pan was plugged into the electric socket under his reading desk, where it was generating a gut of thick steam from boiling samp mealies.

I went to open my window, and not only were the curtains damp, but the windowpane had gathered so much moisture that the wall beneath it was sweating. As soon as I opened the window, my mother's graduation portrait, the laminated merit certificates next to it that were stuck on my wall, and the step-by-step judo poster on the door of his wardrobe, all gently peeled, hung by a corner for a few seconds, and then fell off like a flock of birds struck by lightning on an electric line. I stood there watching the metamorphosis of our living space, while Madoda got up, unplugged the frying pan and retrieved it from under the table. It looked like he was carrying a cloud-manufacturing gadget. He was smiling, paying no attention to me, or the state of affairs in our room, only to his frying pan and its steaming contents – now on top of the reading desk. Then he went to his wardrobe, took out a green perforated dishcloth, and left the room, leaving the door open. I was sitting on my bed, not knowing yet what to say, or even if I should say anything, because I was angry and, I'd realise later, thoroughly entertained.

He returned and looked at me, and somehow that look reminded me that he was a judo sensei. He said, "I fell asleep by mistake, Roomza, otherwise I was watching the pan carefully."

Again, I didn't reply.

I remade my bed, picked up the papers on the floor, and got back into bed without saying a word to my roommate, which was not so smart because as he wiped the spillage from the outside of the frying pan, then its lips, inside and out, he frequently turned to stare at me for far longer than is comfortable to be stared at by a roommate who is a samp-cooking, blind judo sensei. I eventually slept and hoped not to die while leaving Madoda to his mess. When I woke up the next morning, he was eating from the frying pan, once again plugged in, and blowing steam off the plastic fork with every scoop.

But things weren't always that misty in our room.

There were moments where we chatted away for long hours, mostly about religion and family. Madoda is a born-again Christian who is also a lead singer in the ~~Christian Organisation's praise and worship~~

Madoda seemed in quite a hurry to ~~~~ door and close it. He was nervously jiggling the keys in his padlock while talking to me. Normally it is me who rushes off to end our random meetings, to save us both the tension of estrangement. But I'd have done anything to be in the company of my former roommate tonight, rather than worry about a girlfriend who was possibly on her way to the Bellville police station to have me arrested, or worse, crying in a friend's room and spattering her guts out about what she'd call my "history of domestic violence". I greeted Madoda, and we were both surprised, "Roomza?"

"President Zizi."

I wasn't expecting it. I said, "Roomza, you also call me that?"

"You will be the President soon, *mfondin*."

"Two weeks is a long time, Roomza."

"You want to decline?"

"No, no. I have already committed myself to this, but I am saying that in politics a lot of things could still happen in two weeks. It would be embarrassing because everyone's already saying 'President, President'."

"People are preparing themselves."

"Enough about that, Roomza. Where have you been hiding yourself? I don't see you around any more. I even thought you left Ruth First." It was empty talk. But I had to say something to normalise things, bring myself back to the present moment, because I was startled about what might happen to me tonight. Campus Control could appear at any one of the corners of our corridor, and I kept looking around and listening as I spoke. I could only imagine what this short, bespectacled man in his blue Western Province tracksuit would think of me should something like that happen in his presence. I could also feel my penis retracting, and I got all the more irritated by Pamodi's disappearance. Madoda said, "I'm around, Roomza, *you* are the celebrity." He didn't pause for long before adding, "So tomorrow you are presenting *mos*?" He was talking about the presidential manifesto I was preparing. I said, "It'd be great if you came, Roomza. Yeah, it is tomorrow at midday."

"*Hlll*... you are not afraid?"

"I can't afford fear, Roomza."

"Bless you," and if I'd said anything else in reply, and I didn't, he would not have heard it. He was already inside the room, closing the door on me, so that I could only see the black number H-12 on it. I'd felt for the first time the anguish of being alone. I avoid being in the presence of others when something potentially embarrassing is about to happen to me. I isolate myself. I anticipate it alone. And when it does occur, I deal with the outcome alone. But when Madoda locked me out – it felt like he was locking me out – I'd felt very lonely and afraid.

I was hoping I'd find Pamodi in her room. If she was there, maybe we'd come back to my room together and make love. Maybe I didn't, after all, need
[text obscured]
It was a [text obscured], since we're not [text obscured] apartheid universities in the sixties, although they might have been. There are little verandas between the blocks, and the first room on the ground floor of J-block is Pamodi's. It is a double room, which she shares with Mamusa Gqozo.

I knocked softly, composing myself. I didn't want to aggravate the situation with an over-expressive appearance. If Pamodi was there, I didn't intend to give her the idea that I was frightened out of my skull, or that I was possessive, which I am not. If her roommate was there alone, I told myself I'd conceal my desperation. If we cried tears every time we were desperate, streets would be rivers.

There was no answer.

I learned very early on that the silence in this particular room shouldn't ever be read to mean that the roommates were not inside. They never talk to each other. They only have things to say about one another to other people – it's what roommates do on any relatively sane campus. If one day we woke up to the news that one of them had strangled the other to death, we wouldn't ask why; we would know:

Mamusa Gqozo thinks Pamodi is a bitch; she's pretty much told me so. And Pamodi thinks Mamusa Gqozo is a witch, and she is dying from it.

Someone was approaching the door now. It sounded like my brat's feet. The door opened. The girl holding the door had her little pink blankie over her shoulders. She looked at me with unemotional, sleepy eyes. Her face was shiny, her mouth pouting; I'd disturbed her with my knocking. She turned back to her bed. I realised I was still horny, as I stared at her shorts longer than I should have.

Over her shoulder, she said, "My President dude."

"Mamusa, hi. Sorry for waking you."

"You owe me a T-shirt, dude, like literally."

"But you are wearing one."

"I didn't get this one from you."

I assured her I'd bring the political campaign T-shirt myself, and asked, "Are you okay, dude? Seem upset."

"Don't ask."

"Dude, don't give me that, please."

"You can't do anything about it."

"Try me."

"No biggie, dude, like literally. It's just girl's stuff."

"As in *girl's stuff* girl's stuff?"

"Yip."

"Sorry. You'll be fine, dude. Take a pill and nap."

She rolled her eyes and took my advice. She let her body fall sideways onto the bed, and the blanket flipped over her head, revealing her thighs once again. You'd expect a girl to cover up quickly, but she didn't. I stared at her. She looked like one of the strange brown pears found only in this city. My naughty thoughts didn't go far – it was stuffy in the room, and I thought of that pimpled, shiny face under the blanket. She pretended to go back to sleep, giving a little snore, which had the comic effect she intended.

the "girl's

bed, the day

of the bed, and the pointy heels of church shoes the bed. There was no journal on her bed or anywhere else, which meant that she had lied about her friend Melody earlier; she had lied about the poetry session too. That was when I realised I was being had. If Mamusa knew where Pamodi was, she would have volunteered the information.

I still wanted to convince Pamodi to come back and talk it out with me, and possibly make love to bring our bad streak to a close. I wanted to show her that tonight we were just being ordinary, human, and we shouldn't make it out to be more than that; to tell her that miscommunication and jealousy are the normal stuff of couples. I was even prepared to suggest that perhaps I'd let the anxiety of the elections take its toll on me, so that it was now affecting our relationship, and that I wouldn't let my presidency do so once I was elected. I'd then plead for her mercy, and promise a better life for all post-elections.

Since she was not in her room, I feared she was out there with the brush that is her tongue, painting an unpresidential picture of me; and tomorrow I was supposed to convince the masses that for at least one full academic year, I'd be a worthy leader; that they could trust me, unburden themselves to me, and I'd carry their fears and hopes and dreams, and all those intangibles that make them human, with absolute confidence and dignity.

My vision as President would only ever make sense if the masses saw in me the better side of themselves. The masses don't want to see the ugly side of themselves in a leader. That you are handsome, eloquent, have merit certificates on your wall, or are of royal ancestry, and that the organisation deploying you has a track record of producing leaders of moral merit – none of this guarantees hegemony on the ballot any longer. Those credentials used to matter, but that was in the first decade of freedom, when everything was new and no one thought seriously about anything the new leaders said, and before those leaders betrayed students in indefensible ways.

The masses choose you to fight their battles against university management because they recognise in you the courageous, selfless aspect of themselves. They choose someone who could have been their grandfather in exile. The memories of the past regime and the present betrayal are too harsh and too fresh in their minds to be ignored. The masses are searching for redemption. Voters always are. I couldn't possibly emerge as the redeemer tomorrow if my girlfriend was out there tonight telling everyone she had just run away from me, fearing I would beat her up. That it was not the first time it had happened. That she had forgiven me the first time, but couldn't risk it happening again.

That was three weeks ago. We were here at H-14 where we spend most of our time together. If we'd been in love, I'd say we were having quality time, ~~~~~~~~~~ weekend, and I now

evening "Noyana ~~~~~~~~~~

I said, "Someone's at the door."

"How do you know, Baby?"

"Watch."

A few seconds later, there was a knock. The shadows of the knocker's feet under the door had given them away. They could have been comrades coming to consult about a political matter, or student society reps canvassing, and in such cases I don't like being caught unawares. Often I'd need to hide one thing or other – a condom, perhaps – in the wardrobe. This is exactly why all doors in all corridors are always kept shut. I could only see four shadows, which told me it was one person. I was calm enough to let Pamodi open the door, something that I didn't allow when we first started going out. I heard her say *"Hehake* afro..." and then she burst into laughter. Her laughter makes you feel like you are at church and your fly is open.

The visitor turned out to be her friend, Oza, who apparently had a new hairstyle. She had left The Barn, where she had clearly been drinking, to come to H-14 especially to show her friend the hairstyle, and they spoke about it for far longer than I thought it was possible to discuss the matter of naturally kept hair.

They sat on my bed, Pamodi surveying the newly done head, while Oza looked apathetically at me, burping like a beast. I went to sit opposite them, on top of the reading desk, with the stereo behind me and my feet on the chair. I find that I always feel a restrained desire to look cool, swagger, when I'm in the presence of Pamodi's young friends. I hoped my elevated pose would say exactly that.

Later, I excused myself and went to the bathroom. It does concern me that whenever I go to the bathroom, I seem to come back quicker than people expect. It happened again that night, because there was a *so soon?* pause in the room. Oza was eating yoghurt, dipping her fingers in the small pint-size container and sucking them, and Pamodi was munching on smoked viennas, also fingers of a different genre. My girlfriend was saying to her friend, "You're such a witch. You knew I needed to have my hair done, Oz, but you left without saying. How am I supposed to go to the township alone?"

Her face was a register of fear.

The campus population has a curious relationship with the local neighbourhoods, especially the black townships like Gugulethu and Nyanga East, where the likes of Pamodi have their hair done and, while they are at it, get the best homemade foods. The strangeness of this relationship is informed by the terror that was showing on Pamodi's face. Townships frighten the hell out of students, when it is convenient; in the same way that some latter-day urban dwellers claim to fear all that is rural and countryside, even when this is where they were born and bred.

But students can't afford to be permanently fearful of townships, because when vacation time comes, student residences close and students have to go home. ~~The fear is then deferred, to~~

My girlfriend was now contemplating the idea of going to the township alone to have her hair undone, washed and redone. "But Gogo," said her friend (she calls Pamodi "Gogo" – or at times, "Baby" – for reasons I've yet to figure out), "You have *men* issues, Baby, don't forget."

"What's that supposed to mean?"

Men issues is me, I registered. I wanted to hear more, and I hoped Oza's drunken state would allow for this, but thanks to our colonial make-up, hair – like the size of a dick – is more political than any other thing on campus. Oza went on, "Anyway you know very well you can't keep an afro. Last year your hair was better and you chopped it off for no reason," and then she turned to me: "Can you believe she had an afro as big as this last year? She came to my window at Basil February and asked for scissors. Your girlfriend is crazy, Zizi *sana.*"

"You are exaggerating!"

"Don't deny it, Gogo baby," said Oza, and she turned to me again. I listened to her describe the tragicomic scenario of my girlfriend, who apparently took the scissors, chopped off her natural hair in

31

public like a possessed woman, then walked round via NY 1 to the door with a handful of hair and the scissors open in her hand. "You are such a loser."

"Stop it, Oza."

"You can't stop me, Gogo baby."

"I think you should go now, Oz, before you embarrass everyone. You know your mouth leaks when you're sozzled. Go to your room; take a nap. You're getting drunker by the minute."

Oza launched another burp from deep in her guts, and it seemed to stir the hiccups. The mood in the room changed, as hostility brewed between the two friends. Oza was insisting on Pamodi being a loser of unmatched proportions, and Pamodi was no longer amused. She folded herself on top of the bed and hugged Boobsie, her favourite teddy bear, the first one I'd ever seen that actually had breasts. Oza went on citing incidences where her friend had demonstrated this element of being a loser, and even though Oza was, as Pamodi put it, "thoroughly sozzled", it became clear that something else known only to the two of them was hovering in the air.

Unhinged now, burping like a diseased cow, Oza spoke about their first year – last year – when Pamodi had a boyfriend from Pentech. His name was Likhaya. I knew about him. Pamodi had told me Likhaya was her first real boyfriend before me. She knew him from back home in Queenstown. Likhaya attended Queenstown Boys' High School and she went to the girls' counterpart. They broke up after a few months when Likhaya started seeing other girls, and eventually, she started a life of her own on this campus. I knew she regularly bumped into him at The Barn, as there was no drinking hole on Likhaya's campus. That was the end of it, as far as I was concerned, nothing dishonourable about that. But Oza's perspective was ⸺ me; and the sober sense in her led

you so mean.

"You think something happened to me?"

"You tell me."

"You want 'mean'? I'll give you mean."

"Whatever, Oza!"

"Tell us about the laundry!"

"Oh my God, Oza!"

"Zizi," Oza said, "I like you, bro. You're cute, smart and shit. I don't like the other guy, so I'll say this: Likhaya is still around. He's at The Barn as we speak; we drink his parents' money. Gogo does his laundry. You need to put a stop to it." And she burped.

I giggled, but with shock, not amusement. But this was the kind of bad news I needed to hear, as it gave me an invaluable insight into my girlfriend, which would otherwise have taken me a lifetime to gain. "Then there was last year..."

"Fuck you, Oza! Why are you doing this?"

"I'll just go. I'll just..." she sliced the air with the open hand, illustrating how she was to leave the room. She was already on her feet, saying, "You're a loser, shames," and laughing a laugh that said *you're served*. Only now, as she walked towards the door, did I notice

how ashy her feet were. She'd clearly walked across
the sand in Condom Square on her way from The
Barn to here, and she'd been rubbing those feet on my
duvet. This didn't deter me from accompanying her
out of Ruth First, although it was more for me to cool
off than as a kindness to my girlfriend's friend. And I
was confused. She asked me if I knew all this stuff. I
was silent. She said, "Thank me later, Baby."

"Maybe I should thank you now, Oz."

"Oh man, I'm sorry, 'va," and she kissed
me purposely on the lips, a wet kiss that had brutality
in it.

I hastened back to my room to deal with my
shamed girlfriend. She cried heartily for a long time
without saying a word. I watched her emptying her
soul. It seemed as though she was crying for freedom,
not because it hadn't arrived, but because it had. I
decided to not deal with the obvious issue, but to find
out about the unsaid: what had happened last year
that was so big.

She was more forthcoming than I thought she
would be, but not without first halting. "I'm afraid
you won't like me any more. This is probably the end
of us. *Mfxnm*! Exactly what I was avoiding."

There was silence.

I said, "I'm listening, Pamodi."

"Oh my gosh, Baby, you've already decided to
dump me?"

"I haven't decided anything. I'm waiting for you to
talk."

"I will talk," she said but didn't go on. The bags
below her eyes were swollen, and her lips were chapped
from the salt of her tears. I looked at her and may have

moved my hands and eyes to urge her on, but she used her palms to wipe her tears, and then looked at me like she was hypnotising me into compliance. Pamodi could compose herself so well. I admire her for it, but

accompanied by the shrink's speech, "Baby, don't be mad at me *ne*, just think about this: you need to find out why you're easily angered. Sometimes we'll be fighting about something small and I can see I am only responsible for a quarter of that anger you're showing. The rest... you need to find out what that is. Please. For me. Okay? Okay, Baby?" It wouldn't matter how angry I was, when she dished out the shrink's speech, I'd start thinking about my father and lose confidence. If she'd dared start that fucking speech now, I would have exploded.

"Zizi," she said eventually, jolting me back into consciousness, "please promise me two things..."

And she waited.

"I'm not promising you anything, Pamodi. What you need to do is talk, not ask me for things."

"Okay, Baby. *Mamele ke*, I've never told anyone what I'm about to say. My friends don't even know this. Oza doesn't know what she is talking about..."

"I don't want to talk about Oza."

"I'm not talking about Oza."

"Didn't you just say Oza, Pamodi?"

"Okay. I am saying my friends... I didn't tell them the whole thing. They think they know me, but they don't. Everybody in this campus thinks they know everybody else..."

"Are you going to talk about campus now?"

She adjusted her sitting position on top of the bed so that she looked like she was in a yoga class, and then she said, "I didn't tell you that I came back from the mid-year vac last year two weeks late. I was embarrassed." She told me that when she eventually returned, it was with her left arm in plaster, broken, and bruises on her face.

Pamodi's misfortune took place on the second night at home from campus, in Queenstown, where she lived with her grandparents. Her mother passed away when she was twelve, and her aunt Nora and her husband became her guardians. But she didn't like those two.

That morning, her granny had woken her for an urgent family meeting. Pamodi's guardians were in the house, but they had not told her they were coming – yet she had been talking to them on the phone during the bus journey from Cape Town the previous day. They were meant to inform her of the day they'd come to take her to the doctor for her annual medical, and to town for shopping. It had been her first semester away from home, everyone was anxious to see their grown kid, and to hear all about the adventure of a Cape Town campus. But they had planned this all over the phone, and there was meant to be a date for it. The randomness of finding the guardians in her grandparents' lounge told her, before they did so themselves, that something bigger was happening. Her guardian dad was his silent wooden self, and Nora was wearing a melancholic headdress. She began to weep as soon as she saw Pamodi come out of the bedroom. Granny said, "Nora, don't perform *imihlola*. Behave.

first time he'd said the word "adult" to her, she told me. She still thought of herself as a child, but now Granddad was declaring it to be otherwise. He went on, "You are at university. You have proved to us that you are grown up. You have lived on your own for months and you have returned whole. Wouldn't you say that is adulthood, my child?"

Granny said, "Tata, you are scaring the child, *yhini Thixo*!"

The last time they'd been together in such a depressed state, where everybody spoke to her and about her, in her presence, Pamodi told me, was when her mother, Adushu, had passed on from an iatrogenic illness involving her uterus. They had shielded her, but it was no longer possible to keep the truth from her. She was twelve.

She remembers the energetic obsession with which she despised Nora when she was made her guardian. Nora's bras lost their hooks, and her sunglasses lost their screws, and so did her nerves. The destination of one's nerves is the same as that of lost earrings. Nora was a replacement, a substitute, and substitutes are stand-ins for the original. It was the willingness of the substitute to replace that unbalanced Pamodi; yet it is the function of substitutes to fill up the void created by the loss of the original. She responded with ferocious mischief to protect the spirit of the original. The substitute had to climb higher walls than the original just to make the point that it, too, could climb.

This meeting changed all of that. Granddad said, "There is no better way of saying this, my child. Sitting in front of you are your parents: Nora is your mother who gave birth to you, and this man is your father."

Nora had been fifteen when she got pregnant with Pamodi. She was still at school, they told her. The baby was born prematurely. Nora was unwell after the birth; she was overwhelmed, and needed to go back to school. The child was taken by her older sister, Adushu, who was a matron at the local hospital. The elders showed Pamodi the birth certificates: one was the original, which Nora had got after the birth, they told her, and the other was arranged by Adushu. It was easy for Adushu to get it done, given her position at the hospital. There had been plans to make the disclosure when Pamodi turned ten, then twelve; but this was interrupted by the untimely death of Adushu. It had been Adushu who had delayed the great disclosure, they said. She had grown attached to the child, she couldn't have her own. When she passed on, the disclosure was delayed further, and Pamodi's eighteenth birthday was marked as the appropriate time to make it.

She was now eighteen.

She went outside and phoned Likhaya to pick her up. He came in his father's car. He took her to his

home, a few streets from hers. He lived in a flat made
especially for him at the back of the house. He had
a caring concern about him, she said. She hadn't the
~~~~~~~~~~~~~~~~~~~~~~ face the world. But after

he came at her from behind. But
perform, which infuriated him even more.

So he tied her hands to the towbar of the car and
dragged her through the street. She cried for help,
but no one came out. Such screaming was not an
anomaly, as drunks often ended up fighting, shouting
and screaming in these same streets. It was the crack
of dawn, and only dogs responded to her screams. She
was meant to keep up with the moving car, but as soon
as it picked up speed, she'd fall down, and only then
would he stop and let her get up – then it would start
all over again.

This is why she came back to campus a wreck.

It was a terrible crime. It was a terrible story. She
was so young and already she had gone through life's
most horrifying trials. But how could she lie to me
like this!

I decided to focus on restoring her humanness first.
I held her and kissed her on the forehead thoughtfully.
I was pleased when she allowed herself to be engulfed
by me. She was reasonably calm by now, and I was
too. But it didn't last long. I was surprised when she
began crying again. I thought she was crying from

embarrassment and guilt, or tormented by memory, but it turned out she was convinced Oza wanted me for herself, and, to make it worse, I was willing.

"Goddammit, you're such a moron!"

"You left me crying, alone. I needed you. But you went with her. She has her own fucking student card for the gate, she knows her way out. But you went with her. And you don't see anything wrong with it." She accused me of trying to impress Oza by sitting on top of the reading desk earlier, because, it turned out, this position showed the bulge of my penis through my jeans. Oza had remarked on it when I left to go to the bathroom, she said. Her boyfriend was going to the campus gym to "firm up", but clearly I didn't need to, I was "packing".

I lost it. I slapped her.

To make new acquaintances, I let the frog of my chest hop out. I say, here is the frog that keeps trying to jump out of my chest, be gentle with it. I wake one day to find the jumping animal of my chest abandoned, wrapped in a blanket of thorns. I say, be still my frog, I love you; my chest is your refuge, but it keeps frogmarching, and all I can do is follow it, now limping and thudding homewards. I say, stay beloved, you are home. And it does, until the next time it has forgotten how it feels to be sore.

But there are times when I lose my equilibrium at the exact moment the frog of my chest stumbles into thorns. Learning that Pamodi's ex – a man who had violated her and tied her to the back of a car and dragged her guts on the ground – was still in her life, humiliated me. But to be accused of making moves on

Oza sunk a thorn into my frog's delicate skin.

I have regretted my deed for weeks now, but for ᵗʰᵃᵗ duration I have been walking around with an

it hasn't gotten out to the masses so far, but as ᵢ ... outside Pamodi's room, in the porch between our corridors, I had this frightening sense that tonight she was casting aspersions on me. She had probably been waiting for something like tonight, one more disagreement, one more little push, so that she could snap and explode. Tell everyone who I really am; and who better to do that than my girlfriend of months!

If that's what she thought, if that's what she was doing, I had to grant her full credit, *cum laude*, for apt timing. There is no better time to pull a campus politician down than when he or she is running for SRC office. And not just any time or position, but on the eve of the said politician's appearance to the masses as President-elect to make the declaration of his intent. She is out there tonight, I thought, undoing my presidential stature, which was beginning to crystallise in the minds of the masses.

It must have been an hour since she left my room under false pretences. Time moves very slowly when your girlfriend is missing. Thumping beats of house music were blasting illegally from one open window on the uppermost level. Loud music isn't the very best

41

of student residence etiquette. But it wasn't just one lone vagrant who had no sense of campus timing; I could hear the drums the Rastafarians were playing near Allan Boesak. There were students coming back to res from The Barn, from the Dining Hall, from the Study Hall, from Babaz's shop, and random boys gathered in groups, gawking at girls. Res students like gathering at NY 1 in the hope of spotting a headline act of some sort, a mischievous politician perhaps, so that they can corner him or her with a torrent of frivolous questions they don't have the confidence to ask on proper platforms.

I usually thrive during these chance meetings. It gives me the opportunity to connect with the masses at grassroots level. I know the politics of higher education machinery quite intimately, and am usually happy to give a few quick points. But I couldn't bear the prospect of chatting about badly formed policies tonight. I hoped, even though I knew it was almost impossible, that nobody would stop me as I made my way out.

There was another reason I didn't want to talk to anyone.

Before the incident with Pamodi, I had been at Wanga Sigila House. I left at midday, which didn't go down too well with the comrades. I was accused of prematurely abandoning my political responsibilities. I was told I was acting aloof now that I was going to be President of sixteen thousand students instead of just the Chair of our small branch. I was seeing myself as above the collective that had made me. But that wasn't true. I am not a vainglorious jerk. Before I left, I made certain there were enough comrades doing office work up there. We needed foot soldiers to distribute posters and to canvass at the Pedestrian and Steel Park gates, and on Modderdam Road near the

it a point that the office was kept abuzz with activity. By accusing me of high-handedness, I felt comrades were responding to their feelings rather than sensible thoughts, the way my sisters sometimes feel when Mamako kisses them goodnight too early.

I was going to my room to write and rehearse the speech in private. The likes of Sindane rightfully protested the idea, citing tradition, as they hoped to give me the third degree on my speech. This is what we do when there's any grand speech to be delivered the following day by one of us. We don't want comrades embarrassing us in public when we could have been proactive. We listen to the speech and offer critique on the mechanics, content and the taken-for-granted but critical matter of execution. I'd done it before as Chairperson of the branch, and we'd been doing it all week long with the other candidates of my incoming SRC who had already presented. It was necessary for us to assist and probe these candidates as their speeches were portfolio-specific. Mine, however, is meant to be broad and all-encompassing, and it requires a style of its own. I thought perhaps I could make it a long poem. I'm sure it's been done before, if not on this campus, then in places like Cuba and Venezuela and Chile and Mexico, where art is as much of a political device as the gun.

But I had no speech.

I'd decided it would be rather immature of me to write it prematurely. No presidential speech is written five days ahead, because it would be out of date by the time it was delivered. I am talking only about Presidents who take the masses and themselves seriously. A manifesto has to be responsive to the issues of the day, and on our campus, this is literal, although it doesn't seem as if everyone has caught on to this reality. In the last two years I have witnessed presidential candidates sounding like talking pamphlets on the podium, and by the time they reach their last full stop, the Student Centre is empty. The masses have better things to do. I always knew that my own speech was not going to be a personified version of the organisation's election brochure. All the policy imperatives had in any case been addressed by other candidates during the week. I had licence to be fluid. But I couldn't tell the comrades the speech didn't exist at all. I said it was best that I spent the rest of the day "improving" it, and that I should not be expected to be seen anywhere until tomorrow, unless there was a matter of absolute political urgency.

On my way back to res, I saw victory written on the walls. The campus had transformed into a sea of yellow. Wherever you looked, you saw our yellow posters. On the walls of lecture halls, on tree stumps, lampposts and notice boards. The posters had the faces of our fifteen candidates, and me at the centre as their President-elect. Random students who were normally indifferent about campus politics were wearing our yellow T-shirts, bearing our motto for the elections: *Students First.* Yellow is a radical colour, and we were

hardly see her behind the

gogo. Most campus vendors have to put a lot of effort into being nice. They are aware that their lives are in our hands. We have a direct say in who occupies this campus. Mrs Khan knows how to suck up. She was busy serving a crew of very tall white students, who looked like they'd sprung out of a shampoo advertisement.

"The Khans?"

"Hello son, just a minute," and when she saw it was me, "Oh it's you, President. Inshallah!"

I grabbed a roll of wine gums and waved at her. I don't pay at the Khans. The advert boys weren't impressed, but I didn't care. They don't vote; they're the definition of apathy. They didn't know who I was, what I was about, nor did they care, except for the annoying fact that I had overtaken them in a queue without the smallest flinch.

I was now walking past the freshly manicured cricket pitch to my right and the sandy Condom Square on the left, joining NY 1 to return to res. The Barn looks like a funeral parlour during the day. I noticed once more that the roof of the swimming pool was almost complete. When we come back from vac, we'll have a world-class indoor athletic centre right here. It'll be in tiptop condition by the time the football tournament starts.

When I got to res, I met Pamodi and Melody in the foyer. Lately she's been closer to Melody than Oza, for obvious reasons. I didn't think my girlfriend was going far because she was wearing pyjamas and those fluffy slippers that have dog faces. She doesn't normally roam around campus wearing those. When we met at the gate, she was the one who winked and said, "*Hehake,* President!"

It was funny.

I went to H-14, and instead of getting on with the speech, I chose to take forty winks. Naps are crucial to creativity. I remember waking up, checking the time – it was four-on-the-head – and wondering just where the heck my girlfriend was. But there was the speech to write. I searched for the poetry anthology inherited from the outgoing SRC President, in quest of intellectual stimulus, or, to be honest, to emulate the prosaic president of the republic. I gave up on that idea and watched movies instead, to calm myself before I started writing. When Pamodi came back at eight tonight, I had forgotten she had been away. But then came our quarrel, and my search for her, and now I was outside, heading onto campus.

If I am to have any peace of mind tonight, I thought, if I am to write the speech and actually deliver it tomorrow, and if I am to remain a credible President-elect throughout these elections without my image and that of the organisation – and oh God, the mother

body – being tarnished because of my actions, I have
to find Pamodi. I have to go to her friends at Basil
February, where I think she might be. That I could

There are people in green sweaters and
who come in twice per week to water the plants, prune
their branches, and wipe the dust off their leaves. We
are clearly becoming bourgeoisie. Previously you could
see from a distance what was happening in the foyer,
because it has glass walls and glass doors bordered
by thin oak frames; but now with the bourgeois pot
plants, it looks like we are running an undertaker's
business. That is why I didn't see Bonolo Mudau in
good time. If those pot plants hadn't been there, I'd
probably have changed course, or delayed my walk,
whatever it took so that I wouldn't bump into her.

There are not many things I can say about my
corridor-mate, Bonolo Mudau, but I will venture to
say she's the one woman on this campus who, not
by any fault or design of her own, undoes all of my
being in an instant. I stammer and stagger when I
see her, and for a long time afterwards, I continue to
punish myself for staring, stuttering, smiling like an
anxious adolescent, or for having said a stupid and
unmemorable thing. She stays at the opposite end of
my H-floor corridor, which means I get to embarrass
myself more often than is bearable. When I meet her

in the bathrooms, I become overly self-conscious about the fact that the shape of my head is becoming exceedingly oval as I grow older. There's something else rather perplexing that I've observed about myself in relation to Bonolo Mudau: I have never been able to fantasise successfully in a sexual way about her – unlike, say, the way I do about Sthombe. I can only liken this wonder to seeing Mamako or my young sisters naked. Nothing happens that would normally occur just by imagining any other girl in the nude.

Last year, for example, during the June vac, when I'd remained behind to conduct a mid-term review of the outgoing SRC, I saw a random girl's naked body. After the students had gone home, my SRC deployees and I all moved to the smaller res named after Dr Allan Boesak. The morning after we moved in, I was going to their bathrooms for the first time. I was wearing only my boxers and had my toiletry bag with me. I had a bit of a hardness left over since waking up. But it was getting deflated because of the cold. The skin of the male genitals is the best thermometer there is. As I entered the bathrooms, I could hear that one of the showers was occupied, but couldn't say which. There were three shower cubicles. A shower nozzle was hissing in one, and there was steam all around. The one on the far left was open, but I didn't go to it because the floor was too wet and the shower mat didn't look terribly hygienic. The door of the shower cubicle in the middle was closed, and the door of the cubicle on the right was ajar. I opened it and there was the pixy body of a girl: naked, wet and unaware. I stood there for a second without saying anything. I don't know if there's anything to say to a naked girl that is not idiotic. She turned around, and when she saw me, her hands couldn't decide which part of her was most private. I blurted out, "Oh, I'm sorry. I'm sorry."

repeated over the next few days – the delivering, that is. Whenever I see her, I try to look at her with eyes that hopefully say, "No, no, you are wrong. I am not thinking about your body. I can't remember what I saw. Carry on." But the truth is that it's impossible for me to look at Minor Knowles now without imagining the softness of her belly and things below it.

I have various images in my head of other girls on this campus, and they arouse me, but never Bonolo Mudau, not even when she's wearing the rugby shorts she likes. I desire her all right. But it's never a sexual thing, not even when I conjure myself to want her that way. Her thighs, which have this neat soft hair, do not make me want to deliver myself. She is gracious, and it must be that I simply love her, and it terrifies the living frog of my chest.

I met her at the door of the foyer at Ruth First.

I retreated and said, "Oh, ahem, I'm sorry. Please come through, Bonolo."

She made a screwy face as you would to a puppy, and said, "*Ncaaw*. Such a gentleman, this President. I must be a duchess."

"No, this door... I didn't see you. Yes..."

There was a silence. She was smiling in that confused way. She was trying to make sense of my gibberish. I had exposed myself as a jabbering fool once again. I had to save the moment. I said, "I'm not President yet, you know."

"Don't be silly here, *wena*. Tomorrow *ke di* manifestos, *akere?*"

"Yah, that's happening tomorrow."

"Exactly! So you're as good as elected, and you'll make a cute prez too..." she winked and I froze.

I melted the next second and said, "I'll be pleased to see you there."

I wished she would commit to it, but she didn't. I think that if she had, the course of this night would have changed dramatically, and permanently. I believe Bonolo Mudau was created and sent to this university at the time that she was for the sole purpose of showing me that there's always something better to aspire to. But I didn't think like this at that moment, I was thinking about her rather non-committal, "Night-night, Prez."

I didn't have time to mull over the Bonolo Mudau incident any further, and I'd have loved to. Until this moment, in fact, I haven't had time to think about anything in a deliberate way. I was interrupted by the smoker's voice that belongs to our residence manager. She was behind the counter, wearing a nightdress, a thin blue one that made her look like a patient. She had cut her hair, or something, and her spectacles were hanging on the tip of the nose. I was glad it wasn't her husband who was there, because I wasn't in the mood for a long chat about naught.

She spoke first, "I'm watching you, Zizi."

"I can see that, Mrs Hubbs... are you having a good time doing it?"

She pointed at the direction of Bonolo Mudau's

love Ruth First," and I began moving towards the turnstile gate. If Mrs Hubbs had something important to say, she would have put it to me directly. She sees me, and I hope I am not exaggerating, as her third eye – or fifth, if we consider that Hubby exists. Perhaps the correct way of putting it is "critical" eye. She says things to me without any overtures:

"What do you think of my trees, Zizi?"

"Zizi, what do you think of my new House Committee?"

"The Wall of Achievers has grown, Zizi, did you notice?"

I don't express my opinion all the time though, or at least not in an honest way, and sometimes I have no idea what she is on about. On one very rare occasion when I'd been in the DStv room, Mrs Hubbs called me as I came out and spoke to me with a rather worrying conspiratorial tone, "I know exactly who fucks whom on this campus, Zizi. And I know exactly who can't fuck. You kids think you're smart and what-you-call..."

"What happened, Mrs Hubbs?"

"I'm just letting you know. It's part of my job!"

I never really figured that one out. Mrs Hubbs is the type who lets you know she has her nose deeply stuck in your business, and then says it's her job description. Since the incident with Pamodi three weeks ago, I have been dreading what would happen if Mrs Hubbs caught wind of it. The words of disappointment from a parent hurt more than a guilty verdict in a magistrate's court, although I have no first-hand experience of the latter. But she clearly hadn't heard about it. Neither had she heard about tonight's episode, or her blood would still be boiling. "Don't stay up too late, Mrs Hubbs. It is still cold."

"Zizi, what will you do?"

"Mrs Hubbs?"

"I am asking, what you will do about yourself?"

"I don't understand, Mrs Hubbs?" and now I wanted to retrace my steps back through the turnstile gate and get closer to her at the counter. This was going to be embarrassing. "I'm sorry, Mrs Hubbs, what will I do in relation to what?"

She sounded as though she was about to burst into tears: "I have never had a President stay here before. They all go to Dos Santos as soon as they're elected. They want to stay with postgrads. Suddenly they see Ruth First as a what-you-call, a village. Have you decided where you'll stay when you are President? I'd like for you to remain in Ruth First. You've had all your life here, so many of my students look up to you."

"Mrs Hubbs, this is my home."

"I have a nice room for you in G-block. You know that big one in the corner, the student there is not coming back next year. You can have it."

"Mrs Hubbs, please. I'll keep my small room. I'm not going anywhere. You should know something about me: I am not my predecessors." I asked her

loudness of the drums drubbed by Rastafarians at Allan Boesak. They were louder than normal, or things were quieter than usual; either way, you couldn't mistake the drums. If night on campus could be said to have sound, rhythm – and often, a smell – credit is due to our Rastafarians. They are known to explain without tiring that they'll beat the drums till Babylon falls, that is to say, until the delayed but certain total dismantlement of Western political, economic and cultural domination. When I heard the sound, my mind focused only on the possibility that they'd probably had a massive round of *zol* not too long ago, hence their great vigour.

Further down NY 1, a prominent white banner was hanging out of a top-floor window at Chris Hani. It read *Oh Yes*, the catchphrase of the five flamboyant chance-takers who are contesting us in this election. They're not our main opposition, but they serve as an annoyance. I say without envy that they are pretty boys from Joburg, who, I think, find Cape Town and this campus especially boring. When you see them, and observe the showy way they carry themselves, you can't be faulted for concluding that they think our campus is a glorified rural high school, and you wonder why they aren't at Wits, or, if they feel compelled to squander their lives away from home, why they don't go south to UCT or the vineyard in the middle of Stellenbosch.

I've had close encounters with them, or, to be honest, with people who've had even closer encounters with them, and they all tend to agree that these boys feel it is their burden to introduce class to this campus. They're the only students who employ other students to run errands: laundry, shopping, and those in the know say even essays.

But not everyone condemns them. In fact, those of us who are known to dislike their behaviour are reminded that we are youth in transition; we are an emerging elite, aspiring bourgeoisie – that's why we're at university. If there's one thing you learn fast at university, it is to be in two minds about everything. The academy, in fact, is there to modify our strongest convictions and add a lens to our vision. We are told, for example – and we believe it – that if we owned cars, parking space would be top of the list of our priorities. But at the moment most of us aren't drivers, so parking is the least of our problems. Even postgraduation, it takes a long while for one of us to own a car or a house or even simply an account at a retail shop. Our parents empty their pockets, sell what remains of their livestock, and those who can take bank loans, generally having to raise loads of funds on a yearly basis to send their kids to university to acquire education. So for my kind, the acquisition of an education is accidental. What you definitely come out with is heavy financial debt, so that when you eventually qualify and get employment, for a decade you are the least credit-worthy candidate. We are perpetually emerging; the *Oh Yes* boys have "arrived".

There were visitors' shiny cars lining the right-hand side of NY 1. I walked as fast as I could – albeit measured – and tried to not look too intently at the groups of boys and girls who were walking past me. I did the presidential thing: nodding and waving, presenting a smile that each personalised and, I hoped, held on to. One couldn't avoid hearing the whispers of "President" behind one.

There were mating cats atop Basil February. This is their adopted cattery, where you'll see them pole-dancing and sniffing each other's butts. The one being sniffed has to perform a butt presentation to the sniffer. Some are allergic to others; they sneeze endlessly after an attempted sniff. But this is not why we keep them here. This campus is located in a nature reserve. The whole area of Bellville is the result of a nearly successful attempt by the government of the sixties to create a self-governing homeland for Coloureds. They identified this bushy place and erected a college that was meant to be exclusive to that group of people. Thus we find ourselves in a nature reserve in search of higher learning. Some ancestor type decided to collect all the strays of Cape Town and deposit them here to help keep out the snakes. There's talk that they're sterilised. But they doodle, and out of the ten residences on either side of NY 1, the cats seem to prefer Basil February as their doodling spot.

There is another reason Basil February is famous for the art of erotics.

The orgy-prone chauffeur of the outgoing SRC, Congress, stays here. He's a pick-up guy of unrivalled proficiency. He helps our deployees sneak out of campus to go partying in the townships, using the university vehicle he drives. We've discouraged this, but comrades are hellbent on showing off their supposed superior status in the townships. It is a tradition sustained by Congress, as he knows the places and people, and so he keeps passing this custom on from one SRC to the next. He takes comrades to a spot where they will pick up a bunch of – we're told, but we're doubtful – willing schoolgirls, gives them booze, takes them to the beach, feeds them, and at the end of the day, they're brought to Basil February. Those who don't end up in a comrade's room, sleep with Congress, or rock up at a random student's room crying, "My friends left me; I don't know where I am. *Bahambe naba, bhuti.*"

I was part of a group of comrades who asked Congress who these children were. He told us, "Comrades, these teams are members of the Youth League."

"Teams?"

"Yerrs, comrade Chair. They cockblock like a bunch of sardines trying to confuse sharks."

The Youth League is a young people's wing of the

mother body. Together with the Youth League, the Young Communists and the Congress of the Pupils, our organisation forms the Mass Youth Alliance of the Mass Democratic Movement as led by the mother

is, those who do see us at all – as a student wing of the mother body, in reality what unites us with the mother body and its various leagues is subscription to the common principles of non-discrimination, democracy and bias in favour of black people. By nature, a student political organisation is not reducible to one ideology. We are a dynamic beast, shaped in the main by student issues of the day. To have a mother body is contradictory. Because of this, lately, we are being disowned, dismissed as a baseless student platform that can't be depended upon. Undependable because we reserve the right to criticise the mother body, our membership does not *have* to join or vote for the mother body; and finally, because our constituency grows up and becomes labour force for which we cannot account. So we cannot always be trusted to produce future cadres for the mother body.

We are useless if evaluated by the extent to which we can marshal membership for others. If the role of the student movement is to be restricted entirely to producing future membership for already existing organs, then this disables students, denies their agency and hence their duty to define their own future. This is the reason we are not a wing of any particular thing; we are, and will always be, the thing.

As I say, this has led to a paradigm shift. There is a vicious campaign at the national level of the mother body to launch official branches of the Youth League on campuses to replace us. Comrades call it the movement's New Tendency. This New Tendency is out to transform universities into political nurseries for the mother body. The Youth League is seen as part of a looming leadership overhaul, while we're seen as sycophants to the status quo led by the prosaic president. But the current leadership understands our peculiar position: we are ourselves first. The New Tendency cannot conceive of such uncontained vacillation.

Once they've launched branches of the Youth League, they will contest SRC elections. If and when that is achieved, we will be contested on the ballot by our own comrades. As it is, there's news of Youth League branches mushrooming on the KwaZulu-Natal campuses. However, we have managed to keep this New Tendency at bay. I should mention that on this campus, the New Tendency is led by Sindane. This is why he is forever waving a finger at me, saying, "We will meet in Limpopo, sonny," which is where the next national conference of the mother body will be held. He and his cabal are convinced there will be a leadership revamp within the mother body, and the new leaders will make it possible for the Youth League to exist on campuses.

The rest will be history, we're told.

We have legitimate arguments. To begin with, the constitution of the Youth League provides for anyone

under the age of thirty-five to join. Our contention
is that there are members of university staff who are
lecturers, administrators and gardeners who aren't yet
thirty-five. If a branch of the Youth League officially

national legislation states that only students can vote
for and represent other students, and that only student-
oriented structures should be recognised on campuses.
Worker unions cater for the employed. While students
at institutions of higher learning are indeed youth, we
insist that they're a youth of a special type.

Sindane understands this, but it doesn't stop him
from mobilising against us. At the moment, this
contentious issue is still up for debate between our
national leaders. Recent conferences have failed to
resolve it. The likes of Congress, and others who
have access to university resources, exploit this period
of indecision. This is why whenever Congress is
confronted about his orgies with the teams, he tells us
they are members of the Youth League, and we have
no proof that they aren't; given their behaviour, and
his, they may well be.

Congress has been on this campus for years,
creating sex opportunities for comrades at Basil
February. Every time there's a new SRC, the question
of firing him as the driver comes up. But this always
fails to materialise. He has found a way of intimidating

59

the younger chaps we deploy to the SRC. He quickly names members of the great SRCs he chauffeured in the past, familiar names of our ex-cadres who are now members of parliament. So when it comes to the continued employment of Congress as designated chauffer for our SRCs, the conclusion is that he's "the better devil". I have an idea of how to deal with him once I'm elected.

On the door of the room Melody and Oza shared in Basil February was a sign that read *Adult World – No Frauds Allowed.* I stood there, composing myself, so close to the door that anyone opening it would probably freak out and cry for help. I hadn't decided what I would do or say when I found Pamodi. I hadn't properly thought about the state in which I might find her. I had been too preoccupied with avoiding being seen by comrades, and about finding her, to think about what might happen when I did find her. I certainly didn't want to trigger something that could have been avoided by my non-appearance.

Maybe I shouldn't have been there.

I should probably have calmed myself down, returned to my room, and done the responsible thing: written my speech, and forgotten the things over which I had no control. This is something that has been said about me by more than one person: I don't know when to quit. It is probably not true, but if it is, why does it have to come from the ones I trust? I should have quit the relationship a long time ago. In fact, this relationship should have not developed, and when it did, it should not have lasted longer than three months.

The first time I saw Pamodi in my corridor I could have sworn she was Bonolo Mudau. I thought I'd pluck up the courage to declare my love to her. It was a Monday around midday, and the cleaning lady had

"If you ask me twice," she said, or it could have been "nice". I did both, but the shuffling feet made me suspicious, and as she emerged into the light, the frog of my chest was horrified to find out who she wasn't.

I was spontaneous. Spontaneity is a useful attribute on campus. I extended my hand to her, she was not unwilling. I caressed her closer and her entire midriff fitted into my grip like a rugby ball. I instantly got obsessed with holding her up above me like that. It rained all day and night, and I felt her melt deep inside multiple times. She said it was as freeing as an explosive sneeze. I was delighted to liberate her each time. So I was caught in this hypnotic spell from which I had not freed myself until tonight. I should have quit earlier, but I fought instead, and even now that I was searching for her, it wasn't clear in my mind what I was going to do when I found her.

I knocked. There was no answer. I listened and while I was doing so, someone opened the door to the room alongside. Out came a short, stocky lady in a red sleeping outfit – I didn't recognise her, but that could have been her large sleeping headgear. People transform at night. She dashed to the bathroom. I think she puked in there. It was getting late. Ordinary students were sleeping, puking, or about to.

I knocked once more, three quick knocks, and again there was no answer. I left, but this might have been premature. I kept turning my head to see if Adult World would open behind me. It didn't. So I decided I was going to rush to The Barn. If they were not in the room, unless they were at the Bellville police station, they definitely had to be at The Barn. They're not the type to sleep before midnight on any given night. It is a Thursday evening after all, and that's when the hectic drinking starts on this campus; especially now when campus is so jumpy, what with the excitement of presidential manifestos tomorrow, and the welcoming of a new season after a particularly traumatic winter in Cape Town.

I wasn't expecting this – in fact, I was avoiding it – but when I slid out of the turnstile gate at Basil February, I met comrade Styles on NY 1. He was with a postgrad girl. She was leaving him, turning into Eduardo Dos Santos, and he was begging her not to go. She left without turning back. He seemed disappointed, and said when he saw me, "*Thixo*, I think I am drunk! Is that you, President?"

"You are drunk, Styles."

"That's what I am saying, President. I am thinking, no *maan*, I must be drunk; this is not my president. Why is he so thin? I am checking the time, *pltrrrrrr*, I have no watch."

I saw the bottle in his hand and said, "This is uncalled for!"

"But I'm in a party, President."

"This is not a party venue. You are walking on NY 1 with a beer in your hand for the masses to see how responsible my incoming SRC really is. You are doing a great job, Secretary-General."

of choice, and in the thick forest when under attack, I'd be right beside him with confidence, for I don't know anyone who can dodge a bullet better than our Styles. He said now, "Let's socialise a little, President."

"By 'socialise' you mean get drunk?"

"Just a few drinks, President, you can have your Coke, get some food; you need to be fed, President, you are thin. What is the use of a First Lady to the movement if our President is like this? She's lucky they don't vote for First Ladies. She'd be out on a vote of no confidence."

"Where are you guys having a social?"

"I was with these boys up there…" he pointed at the *Oh Yes* window now immediately above us. There was clearly a party happening up there, a party packed with topless young men holding green bottles up in mid-air. "I think comrades are at The Barn. *Kaloku*, I was told President left office early saying he was going to write the speech. I said to the comrades, no *maan*, that's unlike Zizi. He's written all his speeches here, why now? They said no, Styles, this man was serious. He's gone. So I thought to myself no, there's

probably a home affairs matter with comrade First
Lady. President isn't usually like that. He will come
back once that's sorted. Comrades mentioned moods
and all. We sat there and sat and sat and sat, then we
thought no, let's go to res, comrades. We left Wanga
Sigila and I was hijacked by these boys on the way."

"You are unbelievable, Styles!"

"Is President calling me a hypocrite?"

"What are you?"

"I think I'm your Secretary-General, unless you've
changed your mind?"

"I thought so too, but what do you call this?"

"I'm getting to know the enemy, President. They're
just excited kids, ideologically empty, and getting
famous easily with their money. I know them all
from Law, they're not Einsteins. I'm drinking their
booze and I am thinking, yes, yes we need these boys:
they'll make it easy for us to reach the threshold in the
polls next week. After that, leave them to me: I will
neutralise them and absorb them into the movement.
They have a female constituency. Don't take offence,
President, but you don't have much of that. All the
women on this campus are aware of the existence
of comrade First Lady in your life, and they're not
pleased."

"*Mfondin*, those boys are going around campus
de-campaigning us."

"But President... *mamela*," Styles paused. Then
he said, "The masses you are leading are intelligent.
Okay, okay, maybe some of them aren't supposed to
be here, but they are discerning. Look, those boys are
all about sex appeal and cars and sex appeal. Us –
don't take offence, President – we are revolutionaries.

We don't politic via sex."

"That's not strictly true."

"Which part?"

"The sex."

party man. He makes up for his academic weaknesses, preventable lying, and the stringing along of girls by his intuitive awareness and pragmatism. I hadn't wanted him to be deployed to the SRC with me. I argued that one of us has to remain in the branch, if only to keep out the New Tendency. But the comrades said I need a super administrator to balance my politicking, and we could use his popularity at the polls. We decided he would be the "engine" of the SRC, the Secretary-General; and that I would remain Chair of the branch while presiding over the SRC, to prevent the existence of two centres of power.

There were pimped-up cars revving aimlessly, others parked on the street that links The Barn to the swimming pool. There were many more cars around Condom Square. It was dark as usual, and there were pairs of students leaning on each other and against gum trees. Tomorrow the area will be infested with used condoms. It is not Condom Square by accident, and when it isn't, by day, it is a convenient little park with readily available barbeque stands.

When you're approaching The Barn you might feel

that the music is loud, and when you're inside you know for sure it is pumping. This is what I felt when Styles and I entered The Barn. We were searched by the Red Jackets at the door, the famous bouncers who don't give a damn who and what you are, or that this is a university. They're known for brutally beating the crap out of male students, and choking the girls. And yes, they do grab and squeeze the balls when they're searching you, which prompted Styles to say rather too loudly after we were searched, "This your first time, President?"

"For what?"

"The squeeze?" and he gestured. "I see the President cringing and I am thinking no, it must be the first. Their hands are quite something, *Mongameli*. They're like magnets," and while he was still saying that, he saw the owner of The Barn and hailed him, "Hey, David! David? How are you, Chief?" The guy waved at him apathetically. Styles said, "I have the President in the building, Chief; behave," and pointed at me.

That became his theme for the night. When we arrived at the table with the comrades, most of whom were my incoming SRC, Styles exclaimed, "In the building, boys!" After he asked the comrades to make space for me to sit because it was my first time to socialise at The Barn, he said, "In the building!" I shouldn't have been surprised when a tough waiter guy in a black muscle shirt and a Black Label apron came over to our table, deposited a bottle of Jack Daniels and an enamel ice-bucket with champagne in it, and said, "From David."

"Tell David he's a man, he shouldn't bother getting

circumcised," Styles replied. Then he whispered to me, "You should be aware of these things, President, going forward: David's contract is coming to an end in March next year. I sort of told him we'll do what we

let's have this champagne." He looked up and said, "This thing is non-alcoholic *mos*, comrades? Drink, President, as we proceed…"

There really was nothing to say to this, not now, except to make a hundredth mental note to contain Styles's corrupt element during our pending term in office. The table we occupied is the first on the right as you enter The Barn. It is near the food and booze counters, not too far from the exit. It apparently belongs to the Wanga Sigila branch, and nobody chances sitting here even in the absence of comrades. Whenever I came to buy a gatsby here as an ordinary student, I always found senior comrades and convocants at this same table, but I never knew it was permanently reserved. I'd never joined them to stay, but tonight I was finding myself here.

Comrades were talking to each other about Marxism, women, Pan Africanism, and alcohol – exhausting none, but seemingly exhausted by all. Students are a bunch ideologically in limbo, even, or especially, the politicised. Under usual social circumstances, most of the youngsters don't make much conversation with me, but given the excitement tonight at this table, I found myself fielding a few questions about the speech that didn't yet exist – apparently I am intimidating, but what's a bunch of perpetually drunk kids supposed to think of someone their age, with the soul and appearance of their grandfather, who visits The Barn only to buy fast food?

I decided to get up and go looking for Pamodi and her friends in the nooks and corners of The Barn. I hadn't wanted to appear under pressure to the comrades, and the last person I could tell about my mission tonight was the one who brought me to this place. Styles is always looking for people to drag to the dungeon, that is why he kept saying "First Lady, First Lady". I told the comrades I was going to grab a juice. There was a little protest, senior comrades saying the President shouldn't have to buy his own drink, but I vetoed this and for once insisted on getting it myself.

The scene at The Barn essentially features two kinds of tables: those at which one lays out one's glimmering supplies, sits and talk to one's comrades, who are wearing shirts and jerseys like they're important guests at a Christmas lunch, now and then demanding VIP treatment; and the tall tables at which girls in micro-minis lean and get fondled by tall, tough guys in vests. And there were as many tall tough guys in vests, fondling and groping, as there were short-skirted girls allowing themselves to be groped and fondled. One realised immediately that the fondling one spent one's entire youth fantasising about was guaranteed at The Barn. It takes two to fondle: two Russian Bears and two strangers. From here, it is easy to conclude that what happens at The Barn ends up in res. And so, standing there like an ethnographer, observing, one realised that the rate at which girls wake up in beds they don't know is probably much higher than is believed; which means the rate at which sex takes

sometimes walking towards one of them and at other times checking only with my eyes from a distance. There were familiar faces, and strangers; more strangers than known faces in one corner, and in another, my housemates from Ruth First. Nothing looked like Pamodi or her friends. I was temporarily interrupted by someone who recognised me. It was a tall, oldish, very dark guy with very pink lips, and he spoke like he was from Thohoyandou, in English: "What a farce!"

"Are you speaking to me?"

"Student governance is a farce, *bafo*."

"Please excuse me."

He laughed and said, "Political farts!" and he walked away waving his ass at me like it was a chicken's tail. If I was going to have a discussion about the relevance of student governance and flatulence in our lifetime, it wasn't going to be at The Barn, and certainly not tonight. If people had such questions, they knew there were presidential manifestos the following day; they could ask these things there. I wasn't about to shout at the top of my voice just so

I could have a conversation. This is the down side of public life: people think you're public property, and as such are up for vandalism.

I decided to leave. I remembered that Pamodi had left her phone on my desk. There had to be a purpose to that. I wondered what the heck had gotten into me that I had ignored this. I wasn't finding her anywhere, and it was the only link I had to her. I didn't know where she could be. She might still be with her friends somewhere, but I hadn't the foggiest clue where that might be. Perhaps the phone could guide me. Maybe I could even call her friends and ask after her.

I wasn't going to tell the comrades that I was leaving The Barn, even though I felt safe in their company. I didn't want to attract any more attention than I already had. I didn't want to create questions.

That plan failed.

The comrade I was eyeing for the position of Deputy President, and possibly my successor after I completed my term in office, as has become tradition in the entire movement, appeared so thoroughly drunk, she seemed incapable. I'd spotted her from the section of The Barn that resembles a goat kraal, open roof, stench and all. She had been sitting in a corner with men I didn't recognise at first, but who I now saw were the twins who had graduated in the nineties. They were the self-indulgent ex-comrades who found it impossible to outgrow the campus, even with their elephant-size pockets as businessmen in the "real world". They used to dominate our meetings as part of the organisation's convocation, and they were among the instigators of the New Tendency.

But that was before I was Chair of the branch.

I'd never seen them in my meetings. They had been counting on Sindane to be elected Chair, and later President of the SRC, so that they would get the student service tenders for their businesses. And their

Chris Hani, and there'd be fly girls buzzing around it.

Now here they were, propping up my Deputy, taking her out of The Barn. I reacted instinctively and approached them. They were practically stealing her. She wasn't going to be their victim on my watch. She was my responsibility, and it was a presidential thing to do.

I said, "Comrades, is Amaze all right? Are you all right, Amaze?"

They both looked at me with sneers on their bourgeois snuffs, but then carried on as if I wasn't there. I called to Amaze, "My Deputy?" I touched her face and made her look at me.

"President? Fuck! Zizi..." and she began crying, once she had confirmed it was indeed me. She wrestled herself out of their arms and threw herself into mine. David, the owner of The Barn, had come closer and was watching. He had to ensure that his patrons did not get taken advantage of, and that there were no fights. His success was debatable, but the twins were horror-struck, and to save their faces, they left her to me more quickly and easily than I expected. They had

71

to maintain some kind of dignity, and couldn't appear as though they were being dominated by a mere student, especially not about a girl. But we'd already attracted a lot of attention.

Amaze was now saying nonsensical things, crying, wanting to hug me and breathe on my neck, and in the process throwing me off balance. "What the fuck, fucking President! What are you doing here?"

"Don't worry about that, Deputy, let's get you home safe."

"Fuck, don't tell me that after you disappeared all day."

"I'm here now. Let's get you home."

"Hang on," she said. "Listen here..." but she was losing herself into her own jumbled thoughts. We were now staggering out of The Barn. There were people coming in, being searched, and others just hanging around. Immediately in front of us was the university vehicle that belonged to the SRC. There was Congress surrounded by underage, noisy kids who didn't belong here. I told myself that these were their last days in Canaan. There was going to be furniture moving on this campus. "You're taking me home, right?"

"Yeah, let's go, come."

"Listen..."

"Let's talk and walk, come, Deputy."

"Wait, dammit! *'Tsek*, I'm not one of your floozies you can just drag out, *nje*."

Amaze was born and bred in the homeland. She went to school and lived with Xhosa-speaking people her entire life, and this familiarity was part of her choosing to come to this university. We found her to be a revelation. She is articulate and naïve in a way that allows her to cut through the political bullshit and ask pertinent, existential questions. I personally recruited her, and pushed for

world of female majorities. Quite possibly

us and our opposition, which appeals only to certain black Africans, Amaze will be the difference in this election. She has given us that edge. She'll sure get us the much-needed Coloured vote.

I had to take care of her. But when she began speaking fluent Xhosa, I couldn't hold myself, precisely because no matter how used you were to her fluency, it still came as a surprise.

But she wasn't ignorant: "You can laugh all you want. I know you people think I'm your token Coloured and shit. But I am legit."

"Stop with the paranoia, you're my Deputy on merit."

"Fuck merit, don't you also fuck with me. I thought I could trust your ass."

"Well, you can, first by believing I'm not asking for a fuck."

"I'm not one of these easy women you people use as objects... one day I'm going to lead this fucking campus."

"I'm with you there, Deputy."

"One year, not more. One year, and I'm where you

are with no more melanin or dick in me. You know what they say about you?"

I asked her what "they" said about me, but even in her current state, Amaze realised she'd let out something she wasn't meant to. I pressed on with no success.

Amaze is one of those people in my life whom I love to love. I'd like her to be in my life some more, outside politics, in some other yet-to-be determined capacity. Once, when Mamako was talking to me about getting married, one of those random, cringeworthy moments between mother and son, she said as a mother-in-law, she wouldn't mind Amaze. She had only ever seen one photo of Amaze. In it, me and Amaze, in similar T-shirts, are posing in a group hug with four students on Table Mountain. I showed her the photo when I was explaining the mountain trip to her and my sisters. She hadn't remarked on it at the time, so when she dropped the Amaze bomb so suddenly, I was shocked she even remembered the name. It is not every day that my mother embraces a friend of mine like that; in fact, I grew up believing my friends were not welcome to come to my home, so when this happened, the son in me celebrated the presence of Amaze in my life.

Meanwhile, my Deputy was determined to conceal what she'd heard about me, which she now realised wasn't meant to get to my ears. She paused to empty out the sand that had gotten into her shoes. She spoke about her manifesto presentation, which had been a resounding success, and pledged her support as my Deputy. When we got closer to her res, Chris Hani, there was a group of Seventh-Day Adventist guys in suits, harmonising a song a capella-style. They were from Pentech, where there's a vibrant branch of the Seventh-Day Adventist Church.

Amaze sobered up instantly. "This is some shit!"

"W̶h̶a̶t̶?̶"

we greeted and passed them without any ̶

Now that I was seeing these guys, I realised it was already Friday. It was past midnight. I had no speech, and yet at midday-on-the-head, I was due to deliver an election-winning manifesto. My aggrieved girlfriend was still roaming about, and I was increasingly anxious about what might be happening at Ruth First in my absence.

I was somewhat passive for the remainder of the walk with my Deputy. I thought I'd take her to Chris Hani and help her settle and ensure her safety, but now I couldn't wait to rid myself of her. When we got to the fancy foyer of Chris Hani, I said, "Take a nap, my Deputy. The Azanians will be baying for your blood in just a few hours."

"I'm more worried about you, *yazi*."

Normally I'd have dismissed this, told her I was fine, and that she shouldn't worry, but I felt I was in desperate need for a cuddle. I could simply go in with her, and even if we didn't end up making love, tonight would still be memorable. I went to hold her and squish her into me. I felt her brush my lower back, and my hands touched the straps of her bra. She has

75

such large veins on her neck, and they were pulsing. I held her shoulders and kissed her forehead. She put her head on my chest and breathed out aloud. I ruffled her curly hair and let my hand land on her shoulder. I was letting go. At that moment, it felt like the right decision was in opposition to bodily desires. I told her, and it came out unconvincingly, "I'll be fine. I'm a man, Amaze."

"That's so much bullshit."

"It's easy to say when you have nothing to worry about."

"*Kanti*, what's wrong? Tomorrow we're taking this, aren't we? You'll be impressive."

"What would you say if I told you I have no manifesto, and that my girlfriend has gone to the cops to lay a complaint as we speak?"

"I'd say you're drunker than I am."

"You see!"

I told her she might not have a presidential candidate by morning. She might even have to preside over the incoming SRC instead of deputising. I told her Pamodi and I had had a physical fight three weeks ago. It was difficult to admit that I'd beaten up Pamodi, but I said it eventually. I told her that Pamodi had cheated and lied, and that today she had disappeared for the entire day, and when she finally appeared, and I asked her about it, she left me under false pretences. I admitted I had been looking for her all over, and that she was nowhere to be found. As I was saying this to Amaze, it sounded to me like I was justifying violence.

Amaze asked me if, right now, I felt I had to beat up Pamodi. I told her how much I regretted that, and that I truly wouldn't repeat it. I apologised to Amaze as a woman herself, and swore I was already punishing myself.

She listened, and kept asking passing strangers for a cigarette, to no avail. "I'm not saying this to please you

"Listen, Babe," she was calling me this now, "you are clearly rattled. Go to your room; don't be talking to everyone about this shit. Sleep and let tomorrow come. I'll see you in the morning. We'll do the speech together."

She burped.

"Is that it?"

She walked away. I knew there was no way a nap was going to be possible tonight, whether or not Pamodi came back into my life. I realised once more that the nights were still very cold in Cape Town as I hastened down NY 1 to get myself in the room. The light was still on at Adult World, and it was made even brighter by the fact that the lights had gone out in the windows next to it. It didn't look like there had been any change since I'd been there a few hours ago. Babaz's spaza shop was still open, and there were four loud girls arguing about what flavour of pies to buy, and whether or not they were to be warmed. There were cats jumping on top of cars, chasing something or each other. They had shiny eyes and propped-up tails. The windows of the cars were misty, and I noticed there was one more car next to Colleen Williams – Sthombe's silver convertible. The Rastafarians were still beating the drums at Allan Boesak, presumably because there was no indication of Babylon falling to its knees tonight. But it was not only the Rastafarians keeping Allan Boesak alive. There were soft sounds from other residences and joyful voices at peak in Belhar.

When I entered Ruth First, I found I was no longer concerned about Pamodi's motives. She'd made her choice. I had to make my own. This was the vague moment in which I let go of her. I just wanted her out of my life. To think this person could have been the First Lady of this campus!

There was a possibility that I was not, per se, angry with Pamodi, but the age she represented. The generation of our grandparents had lost all rights to self-determination, that of our parents had been of truthsayers, fighters, the age of revolt, ours was of quoting the truth uttered before our time – we truly were in awe of our parents (the brave sadists) – while Pamodi's was a generation of cynics: there was nothing they didn't trivialise. For them, truth was overrated, loyalty a form of self-betrayal of which they wouldn't parttake. Nothing had prepared me to embrace disloyalty, just as it was apparent that she – her generation – was not ready for sycophancy. Is it perhaps the foremost task of the next generation to rubbish what came before? Is our adoration of our parents a failure, and therefore disloyalty a success? My answer to this, my answer with my hands, was disgraceful. She was justified in running away. While this fact did not reflect favourably on me, I didn't need to concern myself about it any further. This is why, when I saw that the light was still on in her room, and even though I thought about going to spy at her window, I decided to head to the broken door of my

untouched. I pressed the power button and the only valuable piece of information was the time: it was long past midnight. I decided to pay a surprise visit to her inbox and sent items, and to my surprise, the phone was locked. It now required a pin code. This was new. Since when had she reactivated the security settings? When we'd just met, I'd discovered by accident that she locked her phone, and I asked her why. She'd said, "I don't want to butt-dial."

"But everybody does."

"So?"

"Nothing, except that cheaters make the same excuse."

"*Hehake*, cheaters! What are you accusing me of *na*, Baby?"

"Let's see," I'd said. "Suspiciousness?"

"*Yhu*! This phone is going to destroy my marriage, *mntw'abantu*..." she fiddled with it and then said, "There, it's unlocked, and now I'm going to dial whoever my bum chooses." When, then, in the course of our relationship, had she decided she was going to lock the phone again? Could it be at the same time

79

she decided she was going to nail me once another argument ensued, tonight being the culmination of such a resolution?

Right then, as I felt my mind starting to ask a million droning questions about the motives of my AWOL girlfriend, I decided to get some work done. Fuck it, I thought. Amaze was correct: let tomorrows bring what they will. My speech wasn't going to write itself.

I flipped open my laptop and typed the routine details that don't require too much thinking when writing a presidential address: the greetings. I went to the past speeches to check that I didn't miss any constituency in my greetings. On our campus, you forget to greet a constituency, a church perhaps, or off-campus students, and you lose votes in their thousands. Most of these greetings were like bad poetry, always addressing the Chancellor in absentia, the Vice-Chancellor and Principal of the university, the Deputy Vice-Chancellors, and the outgoing President and his SRC. I wrote mine, read it out in a whisper, another poem gone bad; I deleted all of it, and decided to tell a story.

I am hearing feet scuffle from the left-hand side of our corridor. They are at the veranda between our H and J blocks. There are no voices, only feet trundling forwards, like fruit falling on a grass floor carpeted with dried leaves. They open the broken door of the corridor and let themselves in. They are waiting for each other. A few seconds pass before the door is closed again. It confirms to me that it is not an individual I can hear, but several people. I instinctively look at the bottom of my door, to see the feet pass. But they don't. They stand, and they move a little to make space for each other. I am seeing their shadows. There are little crooked spaces of light between them. My light inside is dim and the corridor's is bright, so that

if it was an ordinary group, p

have been chatting and giggling and carrying on with a conversation or several; if it was a bunch of drunks from The Barn, they would have been singing or their steps would be staggering; if it had been the guys delivering *The Private Eye* under our doors, it would have been one person who would have switched the corridor lights off, to be as discreet and as quick as possible; but these were ordered steps, and now ordered shadows at my door.

They are knocking.

It is an unhurried knock. It is the kind of knock from someone who is also listening for reaction inside the room. *Nkqo nkqo nkqo*, in an orderly, cold fashion. It is the kind of knock someone would mentally record, so that they can reproduce it at a magistrate's court: "I knocked three times and I listened, your worship. There was no answer. My colleagues and I gave a warning and decided to use force." They have knocked three times and now they are pausing. They are almost certainly gesturing to one other. The gestures are not aggressive. They are slow and deliberate. It is like they are hunters at night aiming at wandering, oblivious bucks.

I have not made any noise. When I came in from The Barn not too long ago, I checked Pamodi's phone, took off my jacket, sat myself on the bed, and picked up my laptop from the floor. It had been plugged in since this afternoon. I had started typing my speech, recording tonight's observations as opening lines, and I was getting fired up. All was silent outside, except for distant Rastafarian noises that I didn't pay attention to. But then I heard the feet. I stopped typing in anxious anticipation. I didn't move then, nor did I when they knocked. I am not moving at this moment. But I know they are gesturing, making signs.

It may be my presidential manifesto at midday, but I don't have the kind of friends who will rock up past midnight to wish me well. I am a senior student; this is my final year, and I don't have that many colleagues – they failed or dropped out – and I don't have any group assignments due, so it can't be my colleagues. I know that it is election time, and therefore door-to-door campaign time, so that one can expect randoms to knock as they canvass for votes. But even politicians have a sense of timing, no matter how inopportune it turns out to be sometimes. We will not be found as a group knocking at students' doors past midnight. My comrades are pompous drunks, I know, but if it was them, I'd have heard a ruckus from NY 1. They'd have fought with Hubby because they would have insisted on him opening the gate for them as they defiantly refused to use their student cards at the turnstile, and if he had refused, one of them would have asked on behalf of the group, "Do you know who we are?" This would have resulted in a major rumpus, which I would have heard from here as I sat writing in silence.

The knockers must be people who have been watching me. They saw me come back from The Barn. They have been following me. They want to either ~~confront me or arrest me. I decide not to get up and~~

~~I stay still.~~

If I don't open the door, I won't know who is there and what they want from me. I won't know if I need to worry or be relieved. But if I open, I might be closing the door to a good chapter of my life. For the second time, they knock. It is a one knuckle, three-thump knock. *Nkqo nkqo nkqo.* I am trying to decide if my waiting hasn't been too long, so that it gives the impression that I am guilty when I do eventually open; or whether it is short enough for me to still open without appearing as though I was hiding something.

There is history to my hesitation. When I was younger, Papako used to make me very anxious when there was a knock at the door. He didn't allow me or Mamako to open the door; he did it himself, and he took his time. If there was a knock and I ran to the door, Papako looked at me admonishingly. My sisters are the same. When there's a knock, they look at Papako, he looks at them, and they look at their feet for five minutes afterwards. When I was their age, if I heard someone crying outside, I was not allowed to run out and see what was happening until Papako had gone to survey it himself and had given some kind of finding, which often came as a heavy sigh if it was danger, or silence if it was something negligible.

If we heard a rare sound, such as the buzzing of a helicopter, I was not allowed to run with the other kids to call for the helicopter to rain sweets. One afternoon there was a helicopter vibrating above us and the kids were chasing it, pleading for it to rain sweets. My dad looked at me with those eyes. I didn't move. I wanted to run after the helicopter like other kids, but I hadn't yet been given permission.

He said, "Mazizi?"

"Papako?"

"What is the matter?"

"There's no matter, Papako."

"Isn't there?"

"There isn't, Papako."

"Do you know what it is those children are after?"

"Papako, they are chasing a chopper," I said, and my dad shook his head. He does that a lot, maybe because he has nothing else to shake his head about, since his greatest achievement in life is to have married Mamako, which is Mamako's utmost failure. Sometimes I dream about him shaking his head at me, and I get sad all day afterwards.

He said, "A chopper, huh?"

"Yes, Papako. It is also called a helicopter. The soldiers patrol with it."

"That's right. But there is something else the helicopter does, do you know that?"

"I don't, Papako."

"Son, on good days like this the helicopter patrols the surrounds and gives sweets to the children, but on bad days, the helicopter rains bullets. You would never

know what day it is. I don't want my children chasing
a helicopter that rains bullets."

Since then, I have had an image of a brown
chopping tank buzzing above us, raining bullets.

seeing how as I am

under my door is similar to how I remember apartheid
knockers – whom I have never seen.

I am going to open the door and face these
unattended shadows. Their presence is no longer
bearable. There is a nameless uncertainty hovering
in the air, and it is tormenting me. Ruth First is not
known for ghosts. If these are people at this door,
I don't need to be supposing. Not opening is only
prolonging the awkwardness. If it is people who are
after me, they may just as well find me. There is no
convenient time to be arrested, or to be ambushed, or
humiliated. I am going to open.

I put the laptop on the bed next to the papers and
close it. If there's going to be a fight when I open
that door, let my laptop be spared. I will still need it
afterwards. I am conscious that I have my clothes on.
If I am being arrested, I will not die of cold overnight
in a holding cell at the Bellville Police Station.

I put my one eye on the spy-hole and it is blocked
by a huge thumb from outside.

I open the door and want to perish. There is a mob.
I move a step back and the frog of my chest thuds

at the sight of the aggressive mob. The leader takes a step forward and speaks, "This whole time!" That's what she says. She is telling the mob as though they are not seeing it with their own eyes, and as though I am not here in front of her. The leader is Oza. There's Melody and the others with her. They look like tombstones: grey, heavy and pained. Pamodi is not among them, but there's the incredibly short figure of Sqojiji – whom I helped gain readmission at the beginning of the year.

I do not respond. I feel I don't yet have permission to speak.

Oza says to me, "Where is the child's phone?"

"Which child?" and I regret this as soon as I say it, because my aim is to make this encounter as hassle-free as possible. But I have just faltered with my reply, and it doesn't go unpunished. Oza says to the mob, "Oh the cheek of this man! You actually think this is some kind of a joke!"

"Are you asking for Pamodi's phone?"

"Oh, there's many? I am disappointed in you, Zizi. I thought you were a decent guy. A person would think you are not like the other politicians. You certainly want everyone to believe that. When they said you were going to be President, I thought 'good choice'. But you know what…"

Oza is giving it to me raw, but is interrupted by Melody behind her, "You are losing the plot, Oz. We're not here for this. If there's to be confrontation, it'll be the cops. Not us. Please hand over the phone, Zizi."

"Well," I say, and I don't know where I get the courage, "here… is… the… phone." Melody thanks

me and tilts her head, and she exaggerates when she
grabs and pulls the door, but she doesn't bang it. If it
was Oza, she would have slammed it shut. I would
~~have preferred the slamming, because this gentleness is~~

doing with my friends, she'd say, "By the time we go to
sleep tonight, you will have been counted in, my boy."
This is how I know they count prisoners at lock-up
time. The mob says I will be counted in. I don't know
if it's a scare tactic, but what is certain is that they have
a say about my future. I am no longer the sole author
of my journey. I have been looking for Pamodi, and
she has been with her friends, letting them in on the
broken side of me. I am no longer seen as the perfect
catch. The "Mister Right" side of me died tonight. The
model of positive masculinity self-mutated tonight,
like a parrot thumping out its feathers. It will take an
eternity to shake off the vicious cloud now hanging
over my head. But there's something I can definitely
do, if time allows: I can write this speech, and if
tomorrow I am still here, I can go up there and deliver
the best presidential manifesto this campus has ever
heard.

It doesn't matter any longer that I still haven't spoken
to Pamodi. The last thing I could have asked her
friends is where she is. She knows where she left me. I

87

will not waste any more of my time chasing after her. She has her motives.

I reach for my laptop and sit on the bed, but there's a thought I can't quite shake off: I can't pretend that I wasn't surprised to see Sqojiji in the mob. I know she is a prominent member of this group, and an almost permanent dweller at Adult World with Oza and Melody and Pamodi. It is not surprising that when Pamodi found her friends earlier tonight, wherever they were, Sqojiji was among them. But when I saw her at my door, I couldn't help thinking, "You too, Sqojiji?"

The first time I encountered Sqojiji was in January, in my capacity as a member of the Academic Task Team of the outgoing SRC. The branch mandated the SRC to form task teams so that each of the fifteen SRC positions had about four non-SRC comrades working in it. This is a most effective way of maintaining a substantive second layer of leadership. It resolves the question of succession simply, and successfully. We are not found wanting when it is time to deploy comrades to structures of student governance. As the Chair, I was deployed to the Academic Task Team because of its sensitivity. Styles is part of the outgoing SRC Secretariat, and Amaze is in the Presidency. Our experience in the task teams makes us the next most eligible group of leaders. The brief for my task team is to assist returning students who have been refused further admission to the institution on the basis of lack of academic progress. These are students who did not gain promotion from one level to the next, for two successive years. They get excluded, for good, and because this is printed on their academic transcripts, they can never be admitted by any other tertiary institution. That is a life signed cruelly away. Every year, about two thousand students on this campus are

more years on this campus than any

she hadn't passed for two years, and had duly been academically excluded. To make matters worse, she kept failing a foundation science course. It is always very embarrassing to fail a foundation course, because you haven't even started the main thing. Styles, who (ironically) isn't doing so well in his own law studies, once put it this way in a briefing session: "Comrades, please, please, this is simple: when they put together these course workbooks, they're thinking: *An Idiot's Guide to Life Science*. If our students fail that, they're beyond idiocy and cannot possibly belong here. As we proceed..."

Styles can be very simplistic.

But when students come to see me about readmission to foundation courses, Styles's words come to mind, and I advise them to go home and think about whether university is where they want to be. I tell them I am aware of the university's rules, which can be very discriminatory, but leaving the university at this stage is probably the best thing for both parties. They could perhaps try a technical college and learn a good trade. We badly need motor mechanics, woodwork merchants, metalworkers and welders, electricians and plumbers. There is nothing shameful about this.

But Sqojiji was my new girlfriend's friend. There was something bigger at play. If I couldn't assist her, her friends would think I was weak, unfit not only for leadership, but the relationship with Pamodi. I had to betray my better judgement. When I asked how she had ended up in this position, she said, "*Hay wethu*, I failed, so what?"

Then she laughed.

I did too, but it was because I was astonished. I told her our next Faculty Student Affairs meeting was the following day, and she should check with me late that afternoon. When I went to the meeting, I still hadn't the foggiest clue what I was going to say to the hostile science committee. It is hard to explain the social complexities of life to mathematicians. To begin with, her case was not even on the agenda, because I had not submitted a letter of appeal. One hadn't been written because there was no acceptable reason why Sqojiji had failed the same courses twice, and she hadn't provided me with one stating why she should be readmitted. But I wasn't too anxious about it; I'd dealt with cases like this before. There were some members of the now outgoing SRC who had been refused readmission, and as can be expected, their cases were much worse.

The tendency towards failure among members of the SRC had led to a very popular campaign in academic circles to depoliticise student governance, and transform it into a system based solely on academic merit. I never risked entertaining this debate in a full meeting. Instead, I prevented the cases of failing SRC members from being discussed by the full

committees, and rather took them to the Deans, who
chaired the committees and could use their discretion
on readmission. When alone with a Dean, I could
always blackmail him or her into submission, or agree

that the said comrade was a struggling

as a student, and thus had no business leading, or being
at university at all. We would have to announce this
shameful news to the student populace. Who wants a
stupid leader? Who would ever believe anything said
by an organisation that had deployed a leader of such
questionable intellect? This wouldn't be well received
by the mother body. The Azanians would milk the
story, and it would be a dark cloud hanging over the
organisation's proverbial head for years to come. A
precedent would have been set, one that would surely
lead to the amendment of the SRC constitution to
add the deathly clause of academic merit. Many of
our current comrades would be excluded from even
considering leadership.

When meeting one on one with the Deans, I
argued that there was much more to leadership than
just academic excellence. Being an A-grade student
doesn't automatically make one the fittest to govern.
The scenario in the country's parliament made my
case strong. Indeed, the scenario of any parliament
or boardroom anywhere in the world strengthened
the logic of my argument – in our era, no country is

being presided over by a professor. It is average former students all round. The academics who are selling the idea of academic merit as a leadership quality to students are hypocrites too, for the same reason: the Vice-Chancellor, Deans and Heads of Departments in the academy aren't the best scholars, and they lead these very same clever academics who want to impose the suspect idea on us. The best lawyers, accountants, doctors, nutritionists out there aren't necessarily those who made it to the Dean's Merit List every year. The single most influential politician in the country, Steve Biko, the founder of our organisation, whose ideological proclivity will outlive any hegemonic regimen, never graduated from any university. After all, the university is a microcosm of society.

It wasn't that the argument wasn't tight enough to be tested by the full committee; it was that this would be a subject of discussion at all. Controversial discussions always get out to the masses, even if they are conducted behind closed doors. Student politics, on the other hand, is all about perceptions. If the perception was created that the SRC was failing, a stain would be painted on us. What stays in the minds of the masses is not whether or not you failed; it is that you were associated with failure, that it was a debate at all – and that was the reality I was avoiding. Sometimes I took on not only SRC cases, but some for which I had no good argument, and depended on the mercy of the Dean. That's how I managed to smuggle back into university a number of shamed students. Some of them have graduated and are functioning expertly in their professions without being questioned. The university proudly refers to them as alumni, and doesn't refuse their hefty donations.

This was how I was going to deal with Sqojiji's case.

Right from the start, when we were adopting the agenda, Professor Kenemeyer from Maths said with a

of his subordinates, who was mocking our private meetings. I addressed myself to the Dean instead: "With your kind permission, Chair, it is correct that I'd like to meet with you separately after this meeting. I also want your opinion on whether it is appropriate for the professor from Maths to joke about a serious meeting concerning students' lives. But we can talk about that when we meet, Chair, if you're available."

"I'll see you, Zizi. Colleagues, let's make this quick and painless," said the Dean.

He was a good man. When he wasn't managing silly professors in this faculty, he was a husband, father and minister at the Methodist church in Bellville. But he was also an ambitious man who didn't hide his aspirations. He wanted to act as Deputy Vice-Chancellor for Academic Affairs, a vacant post that was proving difficult to fill because none of the applicants was suitable: one candidate was an old white man who hadn't published anything of substance since he graduated with his doctoral degree more than a decade ago; another was an opinionated black man whose politics was not aligned with the mother body, and who was famous for "shooting from the hip" in his weekly columns in a national newspaper; and the last was a black woman from Durban whom no one knew anything about other than a few scant biographical facts. The Senate had decided that the post of the Deputy Vice-Chancellor would be temporarily filled by one of the Deans until a suitable candidate had been head-hunted. The next meeting of the Senate was going to vote for such a Dean. The Dean of Science, Professor Seun Damkot, had declared his availability and had been touring the campus to meet voting members of Senate. He was scheduled to meet the SRC as well, because the SRC has seven votes at Senate, and that is quite substantial if you consider that there are only one hundred and twenty members of Senate, some of whom wouldn't attend on the day, or would abstain from voting. And the students' votes in Senate come in a block, which can't be said of any other Senate stakeholder. If you were one of the Deans in the running, and you were clever, you had to win the hearts of the SRC so that when counting your votes, you started with eight. The best way to appease the SRC in January was to be lenient with the readmissions.

So I wasn't overly anxious when I was alone with the Dean after the meeting. He was wearing his usual khaki pants, white shirt, with a black and gold tie from his alma mater, the University of Utrecht, and a matching black blazer. He looked like a farm schoolboy with a balding head. As we moved from the boardroom where the committee had met to his office, he said, "You've become such a crafty politician, Zizi, huh? Guts!"

"Prof, students need competent reps."

"Precisely, precisely! You'll consider running for President this year, huh? Is it coming?"

"That's still far off, Prof. We'll see."

put them back on, clasped his hands, and shifted in his chair. The man was clearly uncomfortable, and I moved on to introduce my case. When I started outlining the details of Sqojiji's study record, he asked if she was one of my colleagues in the SRC. He laughed when I said that the SRC seemed to have learned – literally – a lesson this time. "I have an ordinary student here, Prof. It is quite extreme."

I handed him the document and allowed him a minute to study it. His leafy eyebrows had sweat around them and they moved up and down to create and then conceal the wrinkles on his forehead. He said, "This certainly is extreme."

"I did warn Prof."

"What is your argument?"

"Prof, I think you'll appreciate that some of the students who rock up at our offices do so quite late... so late sometimes that very little or nothing can be done. I think we need to come up with a more proactive programme; that way we can anticipate and even prevent a lot of these cases. Perhaps Prof and his colleagues could advise us on the finer points. As Prof can see, this student flunked the class twice in a row. It is a foundation course, it's a straight NO. As Prof is aware, I don't normally bring things that I think are unreasonable. On the surface, this one seems like such a case. But I've met the student several times, and I've had to think about this more carefully. She could have avoided academic exclusion by deregistering as soon as she figured out she would not be around to attend classes. If we'd known about her situation early enough, we'd have advised her to deregister. Now it looks like she has failed, while in fact she hasn't."

"Oh, she's in trouble this one, Zizi?"

"Indeed, Prof."

"Is she on trial for murder?"

"Not for murder, Prof. It is a different kind of trial, and it's been going on since she registered here the first time. This young lady has had the fortune of being called by her ancestors to be a diviner."

The Dean laughed, but quickly recomposed himself. I continued, "Of course this was not so clear to her at first. She would black out in exams, have these unclear visions and hear confrontational voices, dreams, or faint in class, but the campus doctors and psychologists she saw couldn't settle on a diagnosis."

"Do we have the medical records?"

"It won't be a matter of records, Prof. We don't want to violate the doctor-patient rapport. It will be certificates to say she did consult on the said dates, without pronouncing on the nature of illness. I've sent for them to be organised. If Prof is..."

"Will I have the privilege to see them before the decision?"

"I'll ensure that you do, Prof. Thank you."

I'd anticipated this. The man was simply sticking to the rules. This process required an application to be accompanied by supporting documents. Sometimes ~~...~~ applications for readmission

~~...~~

when he or she was ~~meant to be...~~ and had flunked the first semester courses, at a time when their great-grandmother was in perfect condition. The academics, especially from the law faculty, were so brutal they'd say ninety-year-olds expire anyway, so if anything, this document shows the student is taking the committee for a ride and is being given permission to do so by the clueless SRC.

This was why Professor Seun Damkot was asking for Sqojiji's medical records to show when she supposedly had blackouts. He was sensitive enough not to ask for proof of divination. Not everything in our society can be documented, and not everything should. Once I'd promised to bring the medical certificates next time, he said, "You are saying it is the ancestors who want her out of the university?"

He was looking for loopholes.

"No, Prof. The ancestors don't work against people; they simply require her to work with them, for her own good."

"We could use the expertise of the ancestors on this campus, wouldn't you say, Zizi? When you've been called, you've been called, isn't that correct?"

"Indeed, Prof."

"There's no case here then, huh?"

"Prof?"

"She has been called, Zizi; it follows that she must go."

"Prof, I should explain that being called and accepting the calling is only one phase in the process. It is like graduating with a... a law or accounting degree, it doesn't make you an attorney or accountant. It is your choice whether you proceed to the next phase to become the ultimate thing. She has gone through the process of accepting the calling and has opted to revert back to her studies, which were neglected."

"That they certainly were..."

"With all due respect, Prof, she was not in a position to choose."

"Has she mentioned why she didn't yield to the demands of the elders in good time?" When the Dean said "elders", I knew we were making progress. I told him this was initially as strange to her as I imagined it was to him. No one in her family had ever been sought after by the ancestors. It took a while and several visits to great diviners across the country to know what exactly was involved. I told him that Sqojiji had since accepted the calling and subsequently been assured in her dreams that there would be no such other intermissions. I decided to appeal to the spiritual side of the Dean: "She now has the blessing of the elders, Prof. Maybe Prof would like to meet her someday..."

"That won't be necessary."

"Is Prof sure?"

"Certainly."

"It's a yes then, Prof?"

He sighed and was thoughtful. I seized the moment: "Prof, do you know the current Speaker of parliament?"

"Yes, what's her name? Would she be the lady who

There are a lot of people who have g
this student and the Speaker of parliament have been through. Prof would be amazed. All they need to do is formally acknowledge the calling, but they don't have to graduate into practising diviners right away."

The phone rang.

He looked at the small screen of the telephone and back at me, and then he excused himself. He is an old gent. He pressed a button and we could both hear breathing on the other end. He cleared his throat and said, "Shernice?"

"Excuse me, Prof, y'alls next appointment is here."

"Send him to the boardroom, Shernice. I won't be a minute."

He got up and before he could say anything more, I said, "Prof, give me a YES, pending submission of the outstanding documents. If she fails again for the same reason, we'll advise her to take up divination as a career."

He shook his head. He adjusted his glasses. He grabbed a pink folder from his desk and walked round to my side. I was following him with my eyes. He looked at me over his glasses. He took out a pen from inside his blazer. It was a black gel ballpoint with gold bands at the top, middle and bottom; another accessory from Utrecht. The Dean wrote *Accepted* (and nothing else) at the top corner of Sqojiji's study record, and appended his signature and date at the bottom. I thanked him. He said, "This is utter rubbish, Zizi."

It was.

Sqojiji arrived the following afternoon, without the mob. I was at my desk at Wanga Sigila House, the one furthest from the door. There were two other comrades helping students write their letters and advising them on what supporting documents to attach. The SRC didn't have enough office space. In fact, there wasn't even enough space for the official fifteen members of the SRC, let alone task teams. This was one of the long-standing discussions we'd had with management over years, but in vain. Meanwhile, we used the resources of the Wanga Sigila branch. We could do this, even though ours was a political office rather than a "government" one. There was no contradiction, as long as it was our SRC in power. Only the opposition ever protested this idea, noting that some of us weren't SRC members, but were dabbling in governance issues nonetheless. They were correct, but we were quick to remind them that the SRC was ours. The students voted for the organisation, not individuals. We could recall individuals if we wished, and replace them with new cadres. The power lay with the branch rather than the SRC.

We put it to them that the SRC didn't have the material capacity to run all its programmes in the hectic period of registration at the beginning of the year. It was true. Beside academic readmissions, the SRC had to go through a similar process to represent students who were excluded by the university on the

minute, and so had come crying to the SRC for help. We couldn't join the management in locking them out. We are members of the community before we are university students. That is why we've named the street that connects our residences after the longest street in Gugulethu: Native Yard 1. These are our brothers and sisters. This is us, two or three years ago. Many of these prospective students jumped off the bus from as far as Komga and Giyani with their suitcases in tow and their merit passes in worn brown envelopes. The SRC had to find them academic places, clear them financially, find them accommodation in the residences, and sometimes even temporarily find them food. These students made up an additional five thousand unanticipated cases each year.

We put ourselves in the proverbial shoes of each student. It is unbearable to imagine the reaction of the village family left behind if that smart student had to go back home with the news that *there is no space*. We could imagine the message sent to the community of that student who got excluded because they didn't have enough money, and on the contrary, what it would mean to the young ones who were still school-going, told by their parents to wake up and cross crocodile-infested rivers to go to school every day, if their older sister went to Cape Town to seek further education – and got it. We wanted them to believe. This country needs nothing more. We know who they are.

They are us.

Fifteen SRC members couldn't do it alone. If the organisation didn't come to the rescue, then the SRC would either have to make do with what it had and fail its constituency, or hire robotic, apolitical Student Assistants, who would be intimidated by the unsympathetic academics; or the SRC could just accept our volunteered assistance and be grateful. The debate was never settled. In any event, there wasn't much time for prolonged pseudo-discussions, we had to help desperate students who didn't care one bit where and from whom they got assistance – so long they got an education.

There wasn't much confidentiality at Wanga Sigila House on busy days like this. Comrades had to speak in hushed voices. Once in a while someone would burst out crying on receiving bad news, and we'd have to excuse ourselves until she was comforted; or another student would scream for joy at hearing that they'd been readmitted; sometimes both at the same time. In a moment of hilarity, someone suggested that we keep a gospel song on repeat on one of the PCs, because gospel music is sad and celebratory at the same time.

Our daily schedule was such that we conducted the listening, writing and counselling sessions from morning till midday, went to faculty meetings in the early afternoon, then gave the outcomes in the late afternoons to early evening. We were giving outcomes that afternoon, and I didn't know Sqojiji was waiting in the queue. While I was still crossing out the previous [illegible] sling of her purse divided her chest in half. [illegible] was freshly relaxed and combed upwards, freestyle, so that the ends bent down as though exhausted, and she was wearing shades that covered most of her face. She was sucking a lollipop and when she finally got to my desk she said, "Heeey..."

"Hey, Sqojiji."

"*Yho*, it's busy here today."

"It's that time of the year, Sqojiji."

She was quiet.

I said, "So how are you?"

"Fine, *wethu*."

She didn't ask how I was doing, so I reached for a copy of my Science list and offered her a seat opposite me. She hopped onto the chair with less difficulty than I anticipated. The mood was still tense between us. I hadn't exactly made friends with my new girlfriend's mob. It was easier to joke around and make small talk when Pamodi was present. I said, "So, the good or bad news first?"

"Any news, *wethu* Zizi," and Sqojiji turned her head to admire my past comrades on the wall. I looked at her in contemplation. This person wasn't serious.

She was still wearing her shades and only took the lollipop out of her mouth to speak or gloss her lips. It was like a miniature mic without which she had no voice. She was dangling her short legs in the chair. Here was I holding her future in my fingers, and here was she completely unmoved.

When I give students their outcomes, I contemplate the case and what we've all gone through to arrive at the outcome. I know the unlucky ones. I hug them and encourage them. I come very close to telling them I love them, and sometimes they say it to me in this emotionally charged moment while holding back tears. I tell them with my eyes that the worst is over. Those who wasted everybody's time and told me lies, I look them in the eye and show them their negative results without much involvement. There are also those in the middle who seem unresolved, the troubled kids, lost souls; I spend time knocking sense into them and prescribing therapeutic psychological regimens. I can say confidently that I know how to handle every one of these situations.

But I don't like indifference such as was being demonstrated by Sqojiji, and I don't know how to deal with it. I should not have been surprised by it though, because Sqojiji wasn't the least bothered when she came to see me with the mob that first time.

"Any news it is," I said, finding her name on the list.

"Did you meet Mr Myburgh?"

"Who is he?"

"He is my tutor. *Yho sana*, that one doesn't like me."

It would be safe to say that Sqojiji was not my kind of student to help. I made the consultation quick. I got up with my list in hand, in consideration of her height challenge, and went round to show her that she had been readmitted. I told her the condition was that she should register as soon as possible, and avoid being

~~~~~~~~~~ I may have been rude

"Don't forget it during the ~~~~~~~~~~~~ Sqojiji vowed she wouldn't. Depending on the mood of the student when he or she was leaving our office, we made certain to smuggle the point that this was politics. They shouldn't forget. This was necessary because previously we had been stunned to find some of the students we had helped campaigning for the Azanians. They became our harshest critics, and it was hard to remind them at that stage that their existence on campus was due to us. The students on this campus think that if they are to learn to bite well in the "real world", they have to start with the hand that feeds them. But, to be fair, the behaviour of the comrades throughout the year left much to be desired, and could even trigger opposition.

We had to remind the students now.

I was surprised and not pleased when Pamodi told me that Sqojiji was in love with me. To Pamodi, anyone who has the slightest affection towards me is in love. She said Sqojiji was raving about my help. She couldn't stop talking about how quick and how professional my comrades and I had been. She couldn't believe the SRC and mere students like us were capable of influencing decisions of this level.

The frog of my chest began to hop up to Sqojiji the next time we met. In fact, we didn't meet; I was walking down NY 1 from the office in the afternoon. It was a week or so since she'd come to Wanga Sigila House. I was exhausted, hoping to get to H-14, shower, eat and nap. There was going to be an Extended at eight-on-the-head that night. I had to rest as I was going to chair the Extended, and it required soberness. The sun had not yet slid behind Table Mountain, and it had been a very hot summer's day. The first term had just started, and on my way, I had noticed the new trend of school bags: every other student was carrying their kindergarten satchel. There were pink little Barbie backpacks, others with rabbit ears or elephant trunks flapping on female students' backs; the boys carried their brown or striped briefcases from back in the day. No more slingbags.

I heard a voice call out, "My hero?"

It was coming from the Adult World window in Basil February. Since I met Pamodi, I had grown used to having someone speak to me from that window. It was usually she, and sometimes she was joined by her friends Oza and Melody. They'd ask me to buy them fizzy drinks from Babaz's spaza shop. By the time I reached the counter, the list would have grown to ten items. I was happy to do this. But I knew it didn't make me special in any way. It was their habit to ask any man they knew who was passing by to do the same.

This time it was Sqojiji, and she wasn't asking for anything. I saw her short frame. She was smiling and waving. I waved and smiled back. I didn't think much of it at the time, but later whenever I'd meet her, she'd call me her hero, and from there she never stopped. Sqojiji never elaborated. She never unpacked "hero". She didn't do it with words.

frog of your chest.

A few weeks ago, when I accepted the nomination to preside over the incoming SRC, and as many people congratulated me and started treating me as though I was already President, I found myself thinking of those who would be most pleased by the news. Along with my young sisters and Mamako, comrades, my friend Bomi, Madoda, and my girlfriend, Sqojiji was up there on my imaginary list of loyal supporters. But I hadn't met her since it was made official. I didn't need to. We'd never had a private conversation. All that needed to be said was wrapped up in "hero", which I normally returned with a smile. I was anticipating that when I delivered my manifesto tomorrow, one of the people in the front row would be Sqojiji.

I couldn't have guessed when I opened that door that I would see Sqojiji among the mob. She didn't say a thing. She looked at me and I registered the disappointment in her eyes. It was deep and undeviating. I may have physically assaulted Pamodi three weeks ago, I might have made her believe I'd do it again earlier this night, and I am ready to atone for my imprudence, but it feels like it is the once-inviolable trust that someone like Sqojiji had in me that has been assaulted the most. I know that I am not at liberty to choose whom what I have done violates the most, but I also know what I saw in Sqojiji's eyes. It was shame. For the first time since she had come to see me at Wanga Sigila House, it was not a hero who opened the door to her. The heroic acts have been separated from the person. It is unbearable to think that as I sit here, writing this speech, one of the people who trusted me the most is thinking of me as a violent, remorseless man.

I have failed to be in private what I lead the masses to believe I am in public. I have lost integrity. No, I didn't lose it. I never had it. You can't lose what you didn't have. A stone cannot be said to be dry as though it is in its nature to be wet. I am a man of no integrity, and it has nothing to do with Pamodi. No matter how I look at it, I chose to react the way I did. There were eighty-three other ways in which I could have decided to react, and I chose to slap her, and watched the shock in her face. I have been angry before, and in no other such instance did I react the way I did with Pamodi that night. No one is more annoying than my comrades and the Azanians, yet I've never been involved in a fight with any of them. Instead, I am known for my cool head. I am chosen to lead because of my levelheadedness. So it must be that I lack integrity.

I first questioned my integrity when I was young, growing up in the homeland. I was eleven, and my sisters were wee girls the height of the dog. Mamako

had taken us to visit our grandparents in the village.
She grew up in that place, and since leaving home
for no good reason, namely Papako, she regularly
visited the village. Papako didn't come along. I don't

fish, not bean soup.

At night, my granny sprinkled the cow-dung
smoothened floor with water and swept it with the
short grass broom, so that the dust would not rise.
She was humming a church hymn, bent over, directing
the dirt with care. At our house in town, on windy
days, Papako sprinkles water all over the place, and
Mamako gives him the eye if he brings mud in as
he walks inside. My granny nudged and nudged the
dirt with the grass broom and left it behind the door,
because, "We don't throw our people out in the dark."
That's what she said. When she finished, my aunts
spread the grass mats on the floor and showed me
where I was to sleep. I was the only boy in the room. I
was always the only boy everywhere. I slept alone, and
my sisters slept with my aunts on the other side of the
fireplace. Granny left us and went to the other house
with Mamako and Granddad. She said, "*Goeienag,
kinders.*"

The blankets were rough and smelly and I sneezed
endlessly because of the dust in them. But I got used
to it, and we fell asleep laughing at the stories my aunt
Rita told us about the great mystic called Hempenene.

I thought I was dreaming when I heard, then saw someone pull and then open the door in slow motion. She was wearing a pantyhose head-wrap and a blanket over her shoulders. She stepped out, in slow motion. Pulled the door behind her in slow motion, and I could hear slow footsteps behind the houses. The dogs whined, and then they were quiet. I must have fallen asleep after that, and I don't know how long it was before I felt someone slip behind me. She had a warm body, with rough knees like the skin of a thorn tree. Before I could jump, she whispered, "Sssshhh, it's me."

"Who?"

"Rita."

"Okay."

"Your sister peed."

"Which one?"

"I don't know... sssshhh, let's not wake the others."

"Okay."

"Mazizi?"

"Yes?"

"All right if I sleep next to you?"

"Yes."

Rita is my youngest aunt. She came after Nzuki, who came after Mamako. If this was Rita, then it meant that Nzuki was the one who had walked out in slow motion. Rita was uneasy, shifting, pulling the blankets to her, breathing out, heaping the blankets onto me, sucking in air. I felt her hand on my tummy. She brushed my tummy. She brushed my leg. She slipped her hand into my underwear. I was wearing my red pair. She had a warm hand. She let my thing slip between her fingers, and she wiggled it in slow motion. She tried to open it, but I said "*Hlll...*" and she let it close itself slowly. Then she wiggled it again. I felt it rise and rise. She released it and brought my underwear to my knees. She took off her panties and ~~~~~~~ ~~pillow~~ Then she took my hand and

between her breasts, and it

It happened countless times after that: Nzuki would leave in slow motion, Rita would jump the fireplace, I would remove my own underwear, my thing would open, and there was no pain on the sides of the rearing head. It was sore if I rubbed the hair, or when I was out and the head of my thing caught the breeze or brushed against the rough blankets, but I liked the tickling sensation when I was rubbing inside. We were never found out, and once I grew older, we didn't do it any more. I started to deliver myself. But on her wedding day, which occurred when I was fifteen, Pastor Qololo said Rita had never been touched before.

He was serious.

Pastor Qololo was conducting the ceremony. It was held in the Methodist church, the only building in the village built with rocks chiselled into rectangular loaves and cemented from the bottom up. The church is the biggest venue and the tallest building in the area by far. It was built by the British, for their own reasons. A white flag hovered atop the roof. It was hot inside because the windows of the church are high, up there, and we were down here, deprived of air, and fed up with sitting on wooden furniture all day. Earlier, somebody had seen fit to open the doors to let in some fresh air, but since the entire village was at the church, and there was food all over the place, the dogs from the village soon got into serious bone disputes and started dragging each other by the scruffs, attempting to rip off each other's testicles. It was pandemonium. There was growling and wailing, dog negotiations underway. We could hear it from inside the church. Then suddenly Pastor Qololo went silent; he wore a puzzled look, and he was staring at the door. Everybody turned their heads. We saw one of the wives who was cooking outside – she had on a plastic apron – and as we watched, she grabbed a burning wood stump from under a pot and went after a wailing dog, chasing after it, the dog running for dear life, its tail tucked under, and when she threw the stump at it, she shouted, "*Voetsek!*"

"'*Tsek,*" said the others.

The wailing of a dog is associated with bereavement, and this was a wedding. A young man I'd never seen before in a cream suit and brown tie got up to close the door. Those who had travelled from the city found the whole thing deliriously funny and laughed openly, and slapped each other's hands, while the homeland locals stared at them with bemused faces. Pastor Qololo continued to direct the ceremony at the pace of a chameleon, until he got to the part where he said, rather animatedly, "At this blessed stage, children of the Lord, I ask everyone to pick themselves up, that's right, stand up, if you are already standing, be upright, even if you have arthritis and the high-high and the sugar, get up, stand up, this is a holy moment, oh hallelujah *shiya shiyakgalim shiya shikelele...*" and he spoke the rest of it like that, in tongues, until there was complete silence.

of glory *hangcwele,*

and groom. "All of us who are gathered witnesses to God's truth. Do I hear amen?"

"Amen!"

"You are witness to the union of this untouched bride to this suitable groom. I am going to raise both my hands like this. Are you looking at me? I am going to raise them like this, which means that everyone is standing up. When I bring them down, I want the hall to sit down and be in complete silence. If you do not have a chair to sit on, you are to kneel, or bend, until the moment passes. We are at a wedding, not a School Governing Body meeting. Here is the important part, and listen carefully now: the only person to remain standing is one who feels he has substantial knowledge of a deed that prevents the marriage in holy matrimony of these two souls. If you have knowledge to the effect that this bride is not a virgin, for example, that she has been touched before, or that this man is not suitable, you will remain standing. Once everyone has sat down, you will approach the platform. You will submit by whisper your grievance to the committee of priests on my right-hand side, they are here for that purpose, and they will rule on whether these two are

113

to be joined, or, as is highly unlikely, prevented from marrying today, on the basis of your submission. Now, please, children of the Lord, follow my hands..."

I was standing up like everyone else.

Out of the corner of my eye, I was looking at the held-up hands of Pastor Qololo, but I was also looking at Rita. She was veiled with a little white net cloth. She was smiling nervously. I wasn't. My hands were sweating. In the next moment, the congregation sat down. No one remained standing. Pastor Qololo didn't have the chance to pronounce any further, because someone led the people in a celebratory church song:

Satan has none of the power
That the Lord has;
He does not,
He does not.

If I had had any integrity, I would not have let that moment pass. I cannot go back to that moment to stand up, remain standing, proceed to the priests and whisper the truth to them. I cannot look at my aunt Rita or her husband, and especially not at both of them together. By sitting down with everyone else at the church, I locked my aunt and her husband into a lie. I have thought about confessing, but a lie confessed after the moment of truth is as dangerous as a lie not confessed at all. I carry the weight of that with me. I am heavy with guilt.

But now I have decided I am not going to lock myself into false existence any further than I already have. If I have never had integrity, this is the time to form some. If I am to choose the image of my legacy, it will be of a leader with personal integrity. The picture of personal integrity is a young man standing up while the congregation sits down, walking up to the

In the hours that follow, I hear the melodies of day break. Until then, campus was so quiet you could hear a student's gender change. But now the birds are twittering their dreams to the air, the taxi marshals have started recruiting passengers who may be going to Self-Help, Old Belhar and Pentech, which they creatively mash into one word, shouting it out as Sep-yelp-o'bela-penteg; the others are going to the opposite direction, Sex Circle and B'yavo-b'yavo.

My mouth has gathered the night in it, and when I decide to go to the bathroom to brush my teeth, I am surprised to see that a piece of paper has been slipped under the door. I have been here all night, attentive, and I have been particularly aware of any movement, especially since Pamodi's mob was here, but there is now a piece of paper slipped under the door that I cannot account for. It is *The Private Eye*.

At first, I think this is the most imaginative they've been. There is a portrait of my head, with an enormous hole drilled above the ears. The fissure tunnels through the skull, through what's meant to be my brain, to the other side. It is hollow. The face is blank. Painfully blank, but to their credit, they have got the nose right, although they've stretched the ears too far down, probably to allow for the hole in the head. The skull takes up most of the A5 page. At the bottom, the caption to the cartoon says:

Dear President Zizi,
What a splendid head, yet nothing in it!!!
Yours,
Dr Optic Nerve

It does hurt that the first time I am the sole subject of *The Private Eye*, I have an empty head. But I remind myself that *The Private Eye* is not known for its compliments to politicians. It could have been worse, I know, and it could still be bad later, after they hear about Pamodi from gossip peddlers. I should be relieved, and I am, to a large extent; to a lesser degree, I am offended. But I am holding my splendid head high and I whistle as I make my way to the bathrooms down the corridor.

The sinks are filthy, the small mirrors above them look like they've been spat on, and the thought of brushing my teeth in this mess is nauseating. I choose a shower cubicle that has the least slime on the floor, and run water in it. I don't know if it is only me or whether all men start by smearing soap onto their chests and rubbing until all the hair and both nipples are covered in foam. I like to think of it as a greeting to my body: "Hey, buddy." I let the water fall on the back of my neck and move slowly so that it falls on one shoulder, and then the other and back again, until my skin is numb. I brush my teeth and spit on the floor, run the water over it. I am drying myself now, and then out, and I wipe the mist off the full-length ~~~~or I examine my whole body properly because the

~~~~ me only my face.

~~~ year, once the winter hailstorms ~

a girls'-only fitness club, preferably coached by an out-of-the-closet man. A few weeks later, the campus blossoms with nakedness of various proportions. Whenever there is going to be a big event on campus, the membership of the fitness clubs grows rapidly for about a week, girls shedding the extra fat to fit into the new garments that were bought three sizes too small. The next big event is at midday at the Student Centre, and its main attraction is this President-elect – who is still writing his speech.

As I shift from my sitting position, I am once more reminded of the downside of using laptops. In recent times, I've heard many a laptop user complain about the lack of wireless internet on campus. When I was a fresher, and first joined the organisation, there was a lively "One Student, One Computer" campaign. The campaign became redundant when many of us started buying our own portable machines, and the next chapter of the struggle focused on the accessibility of wireless internet. My own complaint is not that extravagant – it is primitive, in fact – and it isn't the fault of the university: it has been over a year since I became the owner of a laptop, and I've yet to discover the perfect position in which to sit and write for long hours in the confines of my room, H-14. This is one of the faults no doubt attributable to my homeland upbringing; until I came here two and a half years ago, I'd never laid eyes on an actual computer.

As a fresher I was obliged to use the computers at the famous Tintana Lab, along with nine thousand five hundred other clueless students from the homelands. There were not more than fifty computers at Tintana, and there was always a gum-chewing girl with braids standing over your shoulder counting minutes. With the immensity of the pressure to type a two-page essay inside the limit of three hours, the last thing I worried about was my sitting position. I am not certain of the exact moment I mastered the hand-eye coordination that using a computer requires, but it cannot be too far from the time I smooth-talked Mamako into buying me one. It's been over a year now, and to tell the truth, I am still adapting to the laptop situation.

I could not have foreseen that the advent of the laptop would present such serious threats to my health. If I sit on the bed with a bunch of pillows cushioning my back, the laptop where it's meant to be – on my lap – sooner rather than later I feel my lower ribs squeezing what I imagine to be my kidneys out of my abdominal walls. My back makes snapping sounds when I get up. If I sit on the chair and put the computer on the reading desk, very soon my arms, the shoulders and elbows especially, feel the same way I imagine an eaglet does after the day's flying session. My buttocks are not completely flat – they have earned me compliments – and from experience

I can say confidently that they're perfectly spankable, but soon I feel that if I sit on this chair any longer, the ... of my buttocks will drill through the wood. It ... on the floor,

laptop, ... figured out, as I haven't heard ..... complaining about this peculiar problem, and res students are masters of the art of grievance.

I've been on the chair and the desk, I've been on the bed, I've had a pillow underneath my buttocks on the floor, and I've even tried sitting on the window-ledge with the feet on the bed. The comfort of these squatting positions didn't last. As day breaks, I've been repeating some of the squats. On any other given day, sitting all night is not an activity I would volunteer for. Tonight I simply had to do it. I reach for the window and part the curtains, and natural brightness shoots in from outside. There is the lace curtain Pamodi bought me. Until then, I had never thought about the function of lace curtains. Now I know that they help me take the world in moderation. I reach for the fridge and grab a vienna. It is cold and tasteless. I go for more and munch away. I haven't eaten since yesterday, so I forgive myself when I finish the whole packet.

Shortly after this, I hear a ruthless knock. I instinctively look for shadows under the door, but there are none. It is daylight. My mind wakes up to the clutter of campus life outside. I have gotten too absorbed in weaving the vignettes of my life into the speech, and have forgotten that they may still come for me this morning. In my mind, I was going to continue writing in peace, then go to the Student Centre to wait my turn to deliver my address after the presidential candidates of the opposition. Since the mob left, I haven't thought about what might still happen. This drubbing at my door now brings home the fear.

I open the door, and as soon as I do, I am pushed aside by Bomi, who opens my wardrobe, goes for the toiletry shelf, frantically searches, muttering to herself that people delay opening doors as though they are thieves, and now she's going to pee on herself. "Where's the toilet paper of this house?"

"It's at the bottom."

"The bottom of what?"

"Down there."

She grabs a roll and jogs out to the bathrooms. She is not the only girl who has taken toilet paper from my room and run out in the last twenty-four hours. What I have not figured out is what this means. Meaning is embedded in the most unimportant things. We are here to find meaning, and that means we have to exert ourselves in unimportance.

A guy in the corridor whistles at Bomi, and she tells him to jerk off. She's not one for foul language, and it is a pleasure to hear her cursing for once. There is something very depressing about a language free of curses. To speak without foul words is like attempting to drive a nail through a wall with a naked fist; a curse, on the other hand, has the solidity and ferocity of a rock hammer.

She is my friend from Colleen Williams. I met her

in my first year at Cecil Esau. She was in the laundry
room, occupying all the machines, and I was the
[illegible] patiently waiting my turn on the
[illegible] annoyed with her

[illegible]

happened: *[illegible]*
with the pee, and since my room *[illegible]*
to run here. This used to happen often, especially on
Sundays when she came back from church at Pentech.

Pamodi regarded her with suspicion. She told me
there was no way we were not sleeping with each
other, as we weren't related, and Bomi was pretty,
single, had a body to-die-for. "She's your type of girl,
Baby."

"I have a type?"

"Yes," she said. "My opposite number."

When I'd told Bomi about the dazzling idea of "my
opposite number", she gave me a look I was not used
to – a look that made me aware how short she was,
how clear her eyes – and from then on, she simply
distanced herself from me. I didn't have the guts to
ask her what that was all about. I thought I already
knew, but I was afraid to find out what would happen
when I discovered my best friend was in love with me.
I hear it is an essential ingredient in good relationships,
but nobody talks about how one makes the transition
from buddy to intimacy without embarrassing oneself.

Bomi comes back, calmer but still panting, smiling.
She is wearing black tights, a blue bandana, running

shoes with white socks, and sweat forms a South American map on her T-shirt. "I almost peed on myself."

There is a silence.

She sits next to me on the bed, her back against the wall, and the mattress sags down from her weight. She is not an unsubstantial girl. I am deciding if I should tell her what happened three weeks ago, what happened last night. If anybody deserves to know, she does. But she starts talking, telling me it is just as well she was pressed with the pee as she wanted to come and wish me luck for today. She is not coming to the Student Centre. She can't watch those rude people make fun of me.

"Did you see *The Private Eye* today?"

I point to it as it is lying on my desk. She reaches for it and says, "*Kodwa*, Zizi, who writes these things?"

"Probably your friends, the Azanians."

"Can't you sue them or something?"

"Do I look like I have a hole in my head?"

"Let me see..." she touches my head and turns it to the window. She has warm, small hands. "The size is not exact."

"They had to fit it on the page."

"I mean the hole."

The joy it brings me to watch her laugh beggars description. She laughs and smiles frequently, but every time it is a marvel. Bomi is truly a lesson in contentment. She has the kind of joyful personality that would drive sadists into self-destruction. When she gets up, I am suddenly aware of the damp underwear hanging from the rail at the end of my bed. She has seen my underwear countless times – you

do not enter a student's room and come out without
seeing yesterday's underwear – but it is a source of
— the trained eye. She opens the fridge
I'll cook tonight,

Bomi picks up
when she first came in. As she walks to
realise her presence gives me a sense of connectedness.
All along I've been suffering from disconnection. I've
been with Pamodi and my comrades, but apart from
myself.

"I have to tell you something."

"I knew there was something, Mazizi. Are you
okay? Are you okay?" She comes back and puts
a hand on my shoulder and I look at her. I could
weep – I imagine myself doing so, letting warm tears
tumble down the bridge of my nose, not saying a word
afterwards. But I hold myself, and she can see I'm in
turmoil inside. She sits back down next to me: "Do
you wanna talk?"

"I am leaving today."

"Leaving where?"

"I am going home."

"What do you mean?"

"I am tired, Bomi. When I came here, I was beyond
myself with happiness. I'd been accepted to university.
You know, there were kids at my school who were
way smarter than me, but they're not here, they're not
anywhere. I felt lucky; deserving, but also lucky to be

123

among the few who got in – and for the first time in my life, I'd done it on my own, not aided by the family name. I was on my way to being somebody, being a good example to my sisters, making Mamako proud. Every time I raised a hand in lectures and gave a smart answer, I felt good about myself. I discovered I was good with words, spoken and written. But something changed, Bomi."

"What happened, *nyani ke?*"

"Oh, so you agree I changed?"

"You're not... you're not as joyful as you were when I first met you. It's like you're always cautious now."

"I'm aware of that, believe me. I've been up all night thinking, and I find I have regrets. That night when I stood up to the corrupt SRC at the AGM in the Main Hall, I felt good about myself. I was asking all the essential questions, the difficult questions everyone was too afraid to ask. Many people came up to me afterwards to congratulate me for my bravery and eloquence. I felt good – finally I was standing up for something bigger than myself, something that resonated with thousands of other students. When the comrades started noticing me, recruiting me, they found me willing. There was nothing wrong with being part of an unselfish collective."

I ventured a look at her. "Bomi, my father cannot explain where he was during the days of apartheid. When we are old, I thought, my children will meet people I helped on campus, people who were glad to have lived beside me. I was ascending in the structures of the movement, being given responsibilities and exceeding all expectations. When I made mistakes, I was supported and corrected. I was not the only good comrade, but the difference between me and my comrades was that I was clean; there was no dark _____ ʰᵉ ᵘsed against me. Comrades _____ ˡᵉᵃdership

"Next week yᵒᵘ _____ important student on campus. Don't ᵗᵉⁱⁱ _____ afraid of your own shadow."

"The problem with being important is that you are not responsible for it. You see, you don't put your name into a song, and you cannot withdraw it. Someone else does, then everyone joins in, and you are catapulted into this status. Everything you do, no matter how small or private, is illuminated. Your actions and non-actions are put on a pedestal. For you, there is only one context – importance – and everything has to fit into that equation."

She said, "Only you. You think too much about everything."

I ignored that and continued, "At some point, you are bound to make a judgement call that is seen as wrong, that is seen as a betrayal of your importance – you should have known, they'll say; we didn't know he was capable of that. So you live in perpetual awareness of being watched, and you develop a fear of being seen to make mistakes. To be important is an awful existence. It is a trap and most of us, me in particular, walk into it with blind enthusiasm."

"I believe you are exaggerating, my friend. Maybe…"

"That's it: I am living an exaggerated life."

"Maybe it's just the anxiety, *wethu*. You'll walk up there and leave everyone in awe like you normally do. Take it all in with grace. That's what you need to escape this importance thing of yours. I'll pray for you."

"But people who take the status of importance with grace first have to accept that they are important. You have to be very conceited to think that of yourself. If I accept that I am in some way important, then I also accept that there are others who aren't. How do I live with that sort of rubbish in my head? Do you know what I wish for?"

"What?"

"To be good and unimportant."

There was silence.

"So I am going home. By the end of today, I will be free and unimportant."

"Oh-ho!" she said. "Whatever you do with your importance, *wethu*, please do not embarrass me. I am not going to be known as the girl whose friend dropped out and ran away. I'll never forgive you for that, Mazizi. What do you want me to tell your students? Who will stand up for the truth? Mazizi, I am speaking to you as an ordinary student: don't be so selfish. Think about your students."

That's all she said, and she was out.

For the rest of the morning – in this state of reluctant importance – I think about nothing else but the thousands of hopeful students who will be filling up the Student Centre.

It is ten-on-the-head when my phone rings. I have been expecting alarm bells any moment from Wanga

Sigila House, but until now I've been left in peace, as though the organisation has changed its mind about its ... for a president.

... familiar voice. It

"Excuse ...

"It doesn't matter. I want to ask ... question, President-elect, and I promise I will never bother you again."

"Is that you, Vovo?"

"Don't ask questions, just listen."

"Is everything okay?"

"President-elect," – I notice she has stopped calling me "President" – "here is my question for you, and I need a simple 'yes' or 'no' answer: is it your strategy to win these elections by keeping the media and the nurses and your comrades and thousands of students waiting for you? Do you think you are that important?"

"What nurses? What's going on?"

"You are not going to pretend you forgot."

"Forgotten what?"

"You and the other presidential candidates made a commitment to test publicly with the Vice-Chancellor today."

"Oh shit, I forgot this."

"The Main Hall is packed to the ribs, the media have set up, the nurses are ready, the Vice-Chancellor has issued an instruction to start in five minutes, and our President-elect is not there. Should I tell everyone you have forgotten and are pulling out, is that what you want printed in the media tomorrow? Let me ask you this: do you know that you are not yet elected?"

"Vovo, listen, calm down. I am very sorry for this, okay? I'll be up there in a moment, please try to hold things until I arrive."

"Where are you?"

"I am still at res. I've been up all night doing the speech."

"And I am told you are 'the cow that grazes alone'... no one has seen your speech. But then maybe you know what you are doing. After all, a man who slaughters his beast by himself should not be questioned about it."

"Vovo, this speech is not the same as the others, my sister, you'll see. I couldn't give it to anyone to check. Comrades will just have to trust and believe."

"Hehehe! Where have you ever heard of such a thing? If you were not the Chairperson of the Branch, I swear I'd be reporting you, persuading the organisation to recall you immediately for ill-discipline. But you have all the power in the world, and you are making sure we all feel it."

"My sister, please. It's not like that. You make me sound like..."

"Like what?"

"I am not a dictator."

"Listen, President-elect, if you're not here in ten minutes, the show will go on."

"I'll be there in a moment."

"You'd better."

I hear raucous applause in the background at Vovo's end. I dread hearing things about me that are

not meant for my ears, but today is different, and a lot
of shit is being said about me out there, which I feel I
listen, I realise I hear chuckles rather

with the Zs, and, p..
Vovo herself, the performer that she is, was proba.. ,
in the furthest corner of the office, near the wall where
she has calendars of previous SRCs stuck around the
face of Nelson Mandela. She was probably making
faces as she spoke to me, while someone else stood
over the telephone, making monkey gestures at me as
others were bopping their heads laughing.

Vovo's office is always peopled with consorts who
have an unmatched appetite for scandals of sexual and
other forms on this campus – and, in the absence of
new such tales, for prophesying them. Whoever it was
behind Vovo's phone now thinks I am avoiding testing
for HIV. But it is not true. It was our organisation
that proposed this idea. It is part of the *Students
First* campaign. We believe very strongly that if these
diseases are to be overcome one day, students will lead
the way.

When this was agreed upon, my plan was to go for
the dreaded test privately ahead of time, so that when
this day came, there would be no moment of surprise.
Then I discovered my girlfriend was still seeing her
other guy, and then we fought, and the smooth flow
of my life was thrown out of equilibrium. I was

initially so distracted that for a full week, I attended no lectures, I skipped the shower a few times – opting to sleep instead – and my eating habits bordered on abstinence. But in the days leading to last night I thought I was regaining some of my lost coherence.

It helped that I could turn in my mind to the blissful thought of being elected – the idea that the majority of campus voters would, in assured privacy and with all the alertness in the world, collectively decide to elect me ahead of others. But then last night occurred, and my life fell off course afresh, and today the idea of being elected does not rouse the same emotions it originally did. My plan, since I cannot simply pull out, was to get to the office closer to the time of the speech, add a few of this morning's observations in my manifesto, and I'd be ready to hide behind the podium and read. Now I hear that everyone in the Main Hall is waiting for me for other, more frightening, reasons. If I make it to the Main Hall, and if I make it out of it as well – there is a possibility I might not – I imagine we will go straight to the Student Centre, where everything has been set up for the manifestos to unfold.

As I leave H-14, heading towards the Ruth First foyer, I cannot help turning to look at Pamodi's room. The curtains are open, and I can see several girls' heads, all adorned with pantyhose as headgear, around her reading desk, chewing and gesturing to each other with mugs. I turn away in shock. I can't make out who they are – she has lace curtains – and I cannot bring myself to take another look. I am not prepared to face the mob again so soon, or even ever. I am very aware that I am, at this moment, possibly cheating fate.

I feel a sense of relative relief when I reach the reception area. Hubby is napping behind the counter ~~~~ ~~~h open, looking like he fell asleep while ~~~~ ~~~ling into

First, ~~~ ~ ~~ piece of wood I simply let myself be carried ~~ stream to be delivered to the other end of campus. I hurry past all the residences flanking our little brown street, hoping not to meet anyone who might distract me even further. I cannot afford to give the clumsy impression of hurried anxiousness to the masses, who, to make things worse, woke up this morning to the sensational news that I am empty-headed.

I have to keep things satisfactorily presidential.

The only other time I have seen this campus so dejected during the day, without any urgent sign of human life, was when I'd returned to campus too early in my second year, sick of being in the presence of Papako's broody moods, and of Mamako, who came close to begging me to treat my father as I would my sisters. I got off the taxi at the Steel Park gate – noting that I was the only student in the taxi – and stood with my bags, looking at the forlornness of campus, and I could feel the flirtations of depression making an impression. The bluish-silver net fence surrounding the campus had all the remains of Bellville hanging in it: empty trays of chicken pieces, various plastic bags, flapping tissue papers and even Coca-Cola cans trapped by the midriff between the wires. The beige grass was in severe distress. I could see through the trees, which were without the deceit of leaves. In just three short weeks, there was overgrowth on the edges of everything, and the chocolate-brown walls of the residences, with all the curtains drawn in the hundreds of windows, gave me an impression not too different from Valkenberg Mental Hospital.

I have stayed on campus during the mid-year vacation before, and there is always the lone foreign student who can't be anywhere else, or the poor girl from the former homeland who has to earn her tuition fees in the retail shops in Bellville. At other times, the university rents out our rooms to conference attenders, sports confederations and political congresses. There is always someone out there on campus, whether I know them or not; it has never been this empty. Perhaps the crucial point is the most obvious: I have never missed a presidential manifesto, never been late for one, so I don't know how res looks an hour before start time.

With Colleen Williams and Ruth First behind me, I now have Basil February on my right, Dos Santos on my left, then it will be Chris Hani and the Dining Hall on the right, Gencor parking lot and cricket field on the left, The Barn and the swimming pool on the right, with DL and the Khans at the end of NY 1 – and then I'll be at my destination. You can never walk down this lane without bumping into at least eighteen people you know, half of whom will have something urgent to communicate to you. There are some students, guys in general and perverts in particular, who rock up on NY 1 to perform the function of traffic lights. There is always some running commentary behind your back, and at other times to your face.

As a politician you can't establish your popularity on campus without subjecting yourself to the scrutiny ‎‎‎ lly bump into someone,

by thirteen cameras at the tunnel that you ought to pray to make it through.

At the moment there are several gentlemen in navy uniforms, each carrying a white bin with both hands, coming out of Dos Santos and Basil February onto NY 1. They're exchanging the sanitary cans from our bathrooms with ones in the van they came with, and I absolutely have no idea what they do with the hazardous waste.

There are also signs of life at Babaz's shop.

Babaz is leaning over the counter of his yellow container shop, which has a tall tree stalking it from behind. The tree has decided to lean one of its largest branches on top of the container, so that the container looks like a student's head with a pitiable hairstyle. I'll bet none of us senior res students can remember what colour Babaz's container was before waking up to find it yellow one morning a few months ago. Babaz is talking to three customers whose clothing is so skimpy, their bodies are nearly nude. He himself is wearing his legendary communist beret pulled to the side, his grey pullover, and a faded brown short-sleeved shirt. He is demonstrating oral sex, with deft precision, to his audience of three chirpy girls. I don't know them; they're probably from Pentech, in search of remnants of life on this campus. Instead they have found over-the-counter sex courtesy of an aged former communist. This is all we have left of the socialist persuasion: behind every profit there's a transmuted communist. I raise my hand in greeting and he says in return, pointing at me with a banana, "I am the President this side, Com."

Only he knows what he means by "this side". I say, "Viva, Comrade Babaz!"

He raises the clenched banana, which now looks like a toy for adults, and the girls remain attentive to the instructions of the nearly expired communist. I note once again their unfamiliarity. I have seen Babaz do his over-the-counter performances all my campus life, always to consorts who are total strangers to me.

I should have taken the shorter and quieter route that goes behind Eduardo Dos Santos and Liberty, past the soccer and cricket fields, and I'd have avoided Babaz's and NY 1, but I thought of all that sand that always somehow gets into your shoes and socks, no matter how careful you are. I've seen many people, girls going to church at Pentech, walking on the sand as I imagine they would on eggshells, but when they get to the road, they always have to take off their shoes and clean them.

But I am already here on NY 1, and had better move on with cautious haste. The cars that were here last night are gone, the Dining Hall is ghostly, and this makes it hugely embarrassing for me to still be trotting along NY 1. When I pass Chris Hani, I hear a booming voice behind me: "Gov'ment?"

Only one person on the entire campus calls me that. I turn my head and see that he is hurrying to join me. I wait and when he is near enough, I say, "Ch———————, my friend, how are you?"

You say it like it's a ——

"*Na*, no crime, Gov'ment," he says, but I know he has a point, and we laugh. Cho talks about his *dey* girlfriend that I tutored in the first semester, who told Cho last night I'd make a *dey* good president, and that she'd be voting for the first time in her *dey* life.

Everyone around Cho has taken to speaking pidgin. He's like a tunnel funnelling culture from the west to the south of the continent. We are walking past the famous Condom Square, and ahead of us is the Khans, behind which is the DL block, where I was nominated unopposed almost a month ago. Cho is talking nonstop about stuff I have no interest in, but I keep nodding, throwing in blurred responses: indeed, certainly, exactly, that's right. He might be registering a legitimate complaint, or advising his Gov'ment, but I am deaf. My ears wake up to Cho saying, "*Na* this must change, Gov'ment."

I listen and once I hear he is going on about today's edition of *The Private Eye*, a crumpled copy of which he suddenly has in his hand, my ears go deaf again, and, I am sorry to report, I have no idea when Cho and I part along the way. He has probably gone to join the masses at the Main Hall, while I decide to go to the Student Centre. It will help to get a briefing before I launch into the masses. It hasn't been ten minutes since I left res, and I know Vovo Malgas and her giggling comrades are still in the SRC office in the Student Centre, probably gossiping away.

There are boys and girls in pairs rolling on the lawn in front of the Student Centre. They're having the time of their lives and pay no regard to the fact of being on the university premises with thousands of other students. This is not an unfamiliar sight on campus. Wherever there's grass, you're bound to find boy rolling girl mounting boy. I used to pause and watch this rolling and tumbling in disbelief. Now it's as natural a thing to my eye as any other, but nature does take some getting used to.

Pamodi once asked me to hold her hand as we were leaving the Student Centre on our way to res – in broad daylight. She never explained why this was necessary, and I didn't ask. I clasped her hand, and I may or may not have been silent the entire long walk down NY 1. When we got to Ruth First, she told me my hand was sweating, and it was. I suppose I am too far away from rolling on the grass in the middle of campus; I lean too eagerly towards the shy side of normal.

Our Student Centre is a vast dome-shaped theatre with giant glass walls at the back and front, three levels of offices on the right, and shops on the left side. The evergreen lawn on which the students are presently rolling forms a semi-circle in front of the Student Centre, so that when the sun is going down, the shadow of the dome-shaped Student Centre lengthens and traces the exact size and shape of the lawn, similarly to the way Table Mountain's shadow engulfs all of Cape Town at sundown.

The door is open at Wanga Sigila House.

Th̲ ̲ ̲ ̲ ̲ t̲h̲e̲ f̲i̲r̲s̲t̲ thing I notice when I enter the

other colours red and white, while those with my face alone are large and all yellow. It did occur to me that from a distance, my face looks like an oval-shaped stain on a yellow sheet.

The posters are everywhere on campus, mixed with the green and black of the Azanians, the chaff of the independent candidates and the *Oh Yes* boys, as well as the blue Muslims. But here at the Student Centre, there is an entire office papered with yellow, so that when you enter, it is the magnet that arrests your attention. The walls were papered either last night or this morning – and now that I think about it, I'd probably have advised against it, had I been here. Although colour is the language of politics, overstated dominance is nauseating.

I cannot see from here whether there is anybody in the office. The secretary must have opened for the comrades as the other key is with me. All year long I've been first to arrive and last to leave Wanga Sigila House. I am afraid my life has changed dramatically over the last few weeks, culminating in the events of last night, and the comrades will interpret my absence as a symptom of aloofness. But nobody knows what's happening in my life, and the few who do know either do not care, or do not recognise the extent of my troubles. As for the comrades, the only expectation is that I should show up today and not embarrass anyone. I am here, but I cannot promise the latter.

The technicians are busy setting up the stage on the ground floor. Now there is a blast of sound as someone does the mic check. The cleaners, in their powder-pink and blue uniforms, are shining the floor with their machines one last time. There are off-campus students seated at every other table, playing dominos, and as usual they are hellbent on creating the biggest smoke cloud in the Student Centre to date, even though this is a No Smoking area. Up at Aunt Vera's Toast, Let's Go, academics are queuing for toasted chicken mayonnaise sandwiches, and below that, at Captain Dorego, students are coming out with packets of fried fish and chips and coffee in paper cups.

On the middle floor, where the SRC and Electoral Commission offices are located, there are comrades wearing yellow T-shirts sitting at tables, and some are singing in low, mournful voices. It is the revolutionary song about Wanga Sigila, and this creates the promise of a tense political gathering. I was expecting all the action to be at the Main Hall. But here comrades are singing and others are surrounding something on the table, analysing it, with the occasional silence allowing a point to be made and exclamatory gestures afterwards.

When I finally emerge from the staircase, I find the twins at the first table on this floor, the table closest to the SRC office entrance. They are dressed in matching pink-and-white linen today, and they're so clean, their skins smooth, their lips glossed, their beards freshly trimmed – they have to be wearing secret socks, because I see only brown ankles emerging from their suede shoes – that when you imagine yourself in

Until now, and although these are my comrades, convocants of the organisation in fact, I have never had any personal dealings with them. But at this moment I am surprised – and it shouldn't be a surprise – to see them giggling with Amaze, my Deputy. She notices me and quickly composes herself so that she looks like a waitress who is at that table to serve important patrons. For the first time in this election, it disgusts me to see someone wearing a T-shirt with my face on it, and the last person I'd have expected to be responsible for my nausea today is Amaze.

The looks we exchange are those of war.

When one of the singing comrades notices me, he pats another comrade's shoulder, and all eyes turn to me. The singing stops abruptly. At the table behind this one, someone hides *The Private Eye* they've been studying. Since I've been on this campus, since I've been involved in student politics, the appearance of the presidential candidate anywhere where his comrades are present, especially on the day of his manifesto presentation, inspires them to break into song involving his name. It is not so today. Instead, the comrades are reading tabloids that portray me as empty-headed; others betray commitments they'd made to me as recently as last night. This overcomes me, and I am overtaken by such very deep emotions that, clapping my hands in a rhythm, I break into song:

My comrades are full of fear
Oliver Tambo, send me
My comrades are full of fear
Oliver Tambo, send me
I will shoot the bastards
Oliver Tambo, send me.

My comrades are assholes most of the time, but whether or not they understand your motives for singing, or your choice of song, they'll never let you sing alone. And dammit, can my comrades sing! They start to gather around me, and for about two minutes I stay with them in the circle, belting out this emotionally charged song, and then slowly I withdraw and leave them without – I hope – being noticed. I go to the waiting area of the SRC main office, where there's a wooden board with names of the past SRCs printed in gold. Our list should be the next to be printed, with my name at the top. Before last night, it all looked straightforward.

I am not so sure any more.

The outgoing SRC is running on auto-pilot: the incumbent President has been recruited by the Institute for Democracy and Governance as an Assistant Director, which is why the elections have been brought forward. When he told me this in my capacity as the Chairperson of the Branch, of which he is a disciplined deployee, I playfully asked him to repeat the title of his new job. Ever the serious President, he ignored my question, and instead handed me the poetry anthology *Seasons Come to Pass*, saying, "For when

me in smoothly, but I am no longer certain I want him to be present at midday.

I'd been expecting surprise at Vovo's office, explosive comments and laughter perhaps, but when I walk in something else happens: it hops and leaps, the frog of chest. It is shaken, laid down tenderly, and left transfixed. It is the most beautiful, most gentle thing I've ever been in the presence of, and the thought that it might be inspired by me is beyond grasp. It feels like a great unexpected question has been asked. I am looking at her, she is smiling at me, and the other consorts are looking at her, at me, and back at her. It is as though an intense conversation has taken place and consensus has been reached, but there's silence.

The smile that causes the frog of my chest to dance belongs to Bonolo Mudau. She is standing over a chair, bathing Vovo's yellow scalp with some class of hairfood. But I am not able to indulge this moment or edit my speech at Vovo's desk. I am escorted by singing comrades to the adjoining Main Hall, which is, as Vovo had put it, "packed to its ribs". Our song is heard as we approach, the masses come out to join the singing, and although they try to lift and put me on a comrade's shoulder, I refuse. I walk up to join the Vice-Chancellor and the other presidential candidates, who are seated gracefully on the graduation platform. The Vice-Chancellor gets up and gives me an unnecessarily squishy handshake, and then he gestures that we should both smile to the cameras.

Then he takes the podium and requests silence several times – but is completely ignored. My comrades have out-sung the Azanians, drowned them in a sea of yellow, uprooted them from the front rows, and now all one can smell is the whiff of hegemony. The singing evokes the protest spirit, which has now taken over the entire hall. The song is dedicatory:

> *And so we were pleased*
> *To have embarked in revolution*
> *In the company of Comrade Zizi.*

The Vice-Chancellor didn't realise he was walking blindly into one hell of a sacred space. He looks at me for help, and I shrug my shoulders, and it's not out of spite or narcissism alone: some songs are not meant to be interrupted, for some songs embody the students' suffering in all its rawness. You have to be acutely discerning and demonstrative of your allegiance to the cause of the day, or you will be humbled. Now the old man is standing behind the mic, fidgeting with the buttons of his grey blazer. Eventually I get up and approach the podium. He moves and I sing along briefly using the mic, and then proceed to tame the spirit of the house. When I am done, I turn to the Vice-Chancellor and say, "They are yours, Prof."

"I can't be sure," he says. "But thank you."

In his speech, the Vice-Chancellor spreads the disease among students on this campus. In the space of

and individually we are pricked for the dead masses to witness, and the event is captured by well-aimed cameras and scribbled on notepads by dead journalists. No one is willing to receive their results except for the Vice-Chancellor, but no one cares. It is all an act. We've been murdered, and this is our funeral. The Main Hall mournfully heaves itself up and the procession moves slowly to the adjoining Student Centre, where each of the aspiring presidents expects to be hacked to death a second time – this time with words.

But slowly and progressively, words redeem us and the Student Centre comes alive as the masses unite and then do battle in revolutionary songs of yesteryear. The presidential candidates outdo one another and themselves in rhetoric – a parody of the mother bodies. There is no shortage of promises, fantasy or lies. The questions from the floor come from vibrant young minds.

I am the last to speak, and it is way past midday. There are great expectations of me, and my mind is thoroughly rattled, but what brings me back to life – right in time – is a handwritten placard held up by my former roommate. When I see Madoda in the crowd and read his placard as I rise to speak, I feel justified in executing my plan.

The placard says: *Tell no Lice!*

I have returned to Ruth First to add this last part and tidy up the just-read manifesto. I am relieved beyond any saying of it. I will now be handing it to the media, as requested. I have done it. I have made public what is private. It is now all up to the voters, and the question is: are the voters willing to do their part? Exactly what is that? I refused to go to Wanga Sigila House, where the deployment task team – championed by an exceedingly excited Sindane – summoned me to account for what I've just done during these last three excruciating hours. I cannot predict the implications of this final act of defiance. I might be withdrawn as a presidential candidate and expelled from the movement; and who knows, the Vice-Chancellor himself might also have taken exception to my conduct.

But it is not the consequence of truth-telling that matters, it is the act itself. I don't matter (although before last night I did): it is what I have done that does. We will soon find out what the function of truth in politics is.

I am eternally grateful to the commissioners for allowing me to go over the specified limit of twenty minutes per candidate. Granted, no one complained. The rectorate, led by the Vice-Chancellor, sat in the front row for the entire duration. The convocants of the organisation were also in attendance. They could be distinguished by their charcoal suits and red ties. I made no particular eye contact in that direction. The

Azanians and other variations were lumped together in one corner, and there were no complaints there. The rest of the Student Centre was dyed yellow, and neither did yellow raise any objection. They let me be. I doubt the masses would have allowed me to be cut short.

a while the tension dissolved. I felt I'd been granted permission to lay myself bare. The final applause was hesitant at first, but it firmed up and became a standing ovation.

I sped off to Ruth First, avoiding NY 1, and didn't entertain anyone who tried to talk to me about the strange contents of my speech. The commissioners didn't allow any questions or comments – we'd already run over the allocated time by hours – but no one insisted on any. We were all too consumed by the feat.

Pamodi might have been in the audience too, or she might have been at res with her friends, or, in case I believe too much in my own invincibility, she might have left the decision to have me arrested for today. For all I know, she might have been at the Bellville Police Station as I was delivering the address. The shadows will announce themselves in time. Despite how I feel about her, I must thank her for this nameless feeling the remains of this day have left me.

The masses now have the chance to reflect on the importance of what happened at the Student Centre